BONE FEUD

A Novel

WYNNE MCLAUGHLIN

Copyright © 2014 by Wynne McLaughlin

Designed by: Cathy Klein

Cover photo: Colt 1860 Revolver, courtesy of
Rock Island Auction Company, used with permission.

Edited by: eFrog Press

ISBN-13: 978-1502799203
ISBN-10: 1502799200

Acknowledgements

To author Mark Jaffe and his excellent nonfiction book, *The Gilded Dinosaur: The Fossil War Between E. D. Cope and O. C. Marsh and the Rise of American Science*, for teaching me the history of the Bone Feud and starting me on the path that resulted in my own romanticized retelling.

To my friend and fellow author Robert J. Elisberg, who read an early manuscript of this story in screenplay form over a decade ago, and then sat with me in Jerry's Deli in Los Angeles, going over the story point-by-point. He gave me the best and most valuable notes I could have ever hoped for and asked for nothing more than a deli sandwich in return. I'll be forever grateful.

To my mother, Pat McLaughlin, who patiently explained to her five-year-old son that archaeologists don't dig up dinosaur bones, and that he actually wanted to be a paleontologist when he grew up, but if he followed his heart and wasn't afraid of pursuing his dreams, he could be anything he wanted.

To my father, Tom McLaughlin, for firing my

imagination by taking me to the *Harvard Museum of Natural History*, where I first laid eyes on the giant assembled skeletons of these magnificent prehistoric creatures.

To a little orange cat named Garvey, who lent his name and his adventuresome spirit to one of the few completely fictionalized characters in this novel.

And finally, to my wife, Cathy Rae Klein, who inspired the other major fictionalized character in *The Bone Feud* and created the amazing cover graphics. You are my love and my life, and you've been this story's greatest champion from the very beginning. This novel is for you, forever and always.

The following is based on real historical events.

Mostly.

Illustration from
American Naturalist, Vol. 3, 1869

The Fossil Reptiles of New Jersey

by Edward Drinker Cope

Prologue

TIN CUP, NEBRASKA

It's my belief that all of the greatest tales ever told have been told in saloons. It was in such a smoky, heathen-filled den of iniquity that I first heard the tale of the Bone Feud. As with all great tales, it was at its core one hundred percent true. In fact, much of it has long been a matter of historical record. But tales grow in the telling, and I therefore must apologize in advance for any inaccuracies, and beg your indulgence for any romanticized embellishments. I have decided to present the story here, just as it was told to me. I find it entirely too rich and too entertaining to alter, simply to curry favor with pedants and historians.

———

The saloon in question was a nameless establishment in the dilapidated mining town of Tin Cup, Nebraska. In recent years, the local mine had given up the ghost and the town seemed destined to follow. But for now, the residents of Tin Cup were holding on with stubborn tenacity, and on the afternoon of my arrival, it appeared that most of them were holding on in the local saloon.

It was a nameless place, but a place of character, where whiskey flowed, cards were dealt, and Tin Cup's scant wealth was redistributed again and again.

It was early afternoon when I arrived. I pushed through the swinging doors, brushing the stage dust from my tweed jacket, and breathed in the atmosphere with amusement and anticipation. It was a meager crowd, a mix of the unemployed and undesirable, with a table or two of chronic gamblers testing their luck at cards. From a corner of the room, slightly out-of-tune ragtime music jangled from a well-worn player piano.

I approached the bar, where a man in an apron slumped, engrossed in a dime novel. I guessed he was in his late forties by his salt-and-pepper hair. He had the rugged, outdoorsy look of a man who'd done far more in his life than pour whiskey.

"Pardon me. Are you James Garvey?" I asked him.

"That's what my mother called me."

I waited, somewhat impatiently I confess, while he finished the chapter before looking up at me. When he did, he appeared a bit startled, raising his eyebrows at the sight of me: a wiry young man with ginger hair and a handlebar mustache, wire-rimmed spectacles, and—with no thanks to the frontier sun—a blooming constellation of red freckles across my nose and cheeks. His reaction made me blush deeply. I suspect I looked very much like a turnip.

I clumsily shifted the stack of notebooks and papers

I carried from one arm to the other, tugged a business card from my breast pocket, and held it out to him.

"William H. Ballou, sir. I'm a reporter."

He studied me for a moment, amused at my discomfort, then accepted the business card. He gave it a quick once-over, nodded approvingly, and then tucked it into the dime novel to mark his place.

"The *New York Herald*? You're a long way west, Mr. William H. Ballou."

"Yes sir, I am."

"That's to your credit. The frontier does not suffer fools. Please, take a seat."

I planted myself on a barstool gratefully and gathered my papers into a pile on the bar top. Mr. Garvey grabbed a bottle of whiskey and two glasses. As he spoke, he poured three fingers of liquor into each glass.

"So, I'm trying to imagine what might inspire a newspaperman from New York City to travel halfway across this godforsaken continent to visit an unruly piss-hole like Tin Cup. I must confide, I am most definitely at a loss."

I tested a sip of the whiskey, which was not entirely unpalatable, and felt its warm glow spread from my belly. It settled my nervousness and stirred my investigative spirit.

"Well, frankly . . . I came to see you, sir."

This brought a belly laugh. "Me?"

"Yes sir, that is a fact. It is my understanding that you once worked as a guide for the renowned paleontologist, Professor Edward Cope."

He smiled, his eyes brightening. "Once upon a time, I

surely did." He toasted silently and downed the remainder of his whiskey.

"If you're willing, I'd like to ask you some questions for a story I'm working on."

He refilled his glass, the wistful smile never leaving his face, and finished my thought. "About the feud with Professor Marsh."

"Yes, that's right. Exactly."

He lifted the glass, sipping this time.

"Well, now. It's been written up six ways from Sunday. I even hear there's a dime novel version."

"I want the real story, the one that won't make it into the history books or the scientific journals."

"And you think I'm the man to tell it, do you?"

"If you were actually there, you are most definitely the person to tell it. You're absolutely right. There have been plenty of stories. The trouble is, every account is different. Most of them are second or third hand. I don't know . . . I guess I figured, maybe since you weren't in such a rush to tell your version, it might be the closest to the truth."

Garvey chuckled heartily. "Well, I can't argue with that logic, son. Despite my choice of reading materials . . ." he nodded towards the adventure novel he'd set down, a recent translation of the French novel by Jules Verne, *A Journey to the Center of the Earth*, "I've never been one for unnecessary embellishment. You want the God's honest truth? In this particular case, there's no need. It's a hell of a goddamn story."

I was already flipping open a notebook and licking the tip of a sharpened pencil to take notes. I may have been salivating.

"I would love to hear it."

"All right. Well . . ." He tugged a leather pouch from his pocket, sprinkled tobacco into the folds of a cigarette paper, and began to twist it into shape. "As far as history books and newspapers are concerned . . . and no offense intended, Mr. William H. Ballou, *Ace Reporter* . . . but, it's my belief that they are not to be trusted. I think history is just an interpretation of events, intended to justify the deeds of the people in power." He paused for a moment, considering. "I guess memory's like that too, on a smaller scale." He paused to lick the cigarette paper and seal it. "What I'm saying, son, is don't expect complete accuracy from me, or the books. The truth is bound to be somewhere in between."

"I'd like to hear it the way you remember it."

"Well now, everybody talks about what happened at Como Bluff. That certainly was where things got out of hand. But, to understand it all, you got to go back a bit further." He caught the cigarette in his lip, deftly, and struck a wooden match to it.

"For me," he continued, waving the match in a lazy arc to extinguish it, "it started the year before, on a stage out of Helena, Montana, bound for Fort Benton. That's where I first met Professor Edward Drinker Cope."

Chapter One

MONTANA TERRITORY

"This was a monstrous animal!"

Professor Cope rummaged excitedly through the leather satchel at his feet as the stagecoach swayed and lurched, its metal-banded wheels catching along ruts of hardened mud. He produced a rolled-up parchment and unfurled it across his young assistant's lap, nearly knocking the bowler cap from Sternberg's head in the process.

"It had a skull at least three feet long. Hips, five feet across." On the parchment was a rough sketch, done in charcoal, of an animal skeleton. "Shorter legs than an elephant. More like a rhinoceros, but twice the size!"

Edward Drinker Cope was in his mid-thirties, tall and angular, with a pleasant, vaguely handsome face that burned with passion and excitement as he spoke. Charles Hazelius Sternberg was ten years younger, with a durably boyish face and bright, intelligent eyes. He couldn't help but get swept up in his mentor's enthusiasm.

"Incredible! What do you call it?"

"*Eobasileus cornutus*."

Sternberg nodded his approval. "Crowned dawn-king. Very majestic."

In the seat across from them, a pinched-faced older man in preacher garb shook his head derisively and made a show of returning to the intense study of his dog-eared Bible. A young cowboy sat beside the preacher, Stetson pushed back on his head, hands folded across his chest, watching the entire scene with amusement.

"The one that got away, huh?" said the cowboy. "Nice of you to give him a name."

Cope looked up. "Would you like to see?"

"Why not?"

The cowboy leaned forward as Cope spun the diagram around to give him a better view. If this was the skeleton of a real creature, it was like nothing he'd ever seen. It was massive and multi-horned. Almost rhinoceros-like.

"Holy goddamn!" the cowboy exclaimed. "I'd be sure to drink upstream of a herd of them."

Cope laughed. "I wouldn't worry yourself, my friend. *Eobasileus* has been extinct for thirty-seven million years."

At this, the preacher could no longer contain himself. "Nonsense! Utter nonsense!"

"Nonsense?" asked Cope.

"The archbishop James Ussher, using the Holy Bible itself, worked back generation by generation, mathematically, and calculated that the Earth was created on Sunday, October 23, 4004 BC at precisely eight a.m."

"Did he, now? Eight a.m., precisely?"

"Precisely," the preacher insisted.

Cope and Sternberg exchanged amused looks.

"Well," Cope replied, "since the rotation of the Earth assures us that it's always eight a.m. somewhere in the world, I suppose I should applaud him for guessing the correct time, at least."

The cowboy couldn't help but interject.

"Pardon me, Preacher, but if I recall correctly, didn't the Bible say something about the Lord resting on the seventh day?"

The preacher looked confused. "What?"

"I'm certain of it." The cowboy quickly snatched the Bible from the preacher's hands and opened it to the first page of Genesis. "Sure. Here it is. He got started on a Monday, making light and darkness. By the time he got around to creating the Earth it was well into the third day. I make that to be Wednesday, not Sunday."

Nonplussed and blushing, the preacher snatched his Bible back.

The cowboy shrugged. "Looks to me like your archbishop pulled a fast one, Preacher. Or maybe he just wasn't all that good at calculating."

Sternberg choked on his involuntary laughter and unsuccessfully tried to disguise it with a cough. The old man frowned and lifted the Bible to cover his blush. Cope beamed and pulled a silver flask from his pocket, offering it to the cowboy.

"Well played, sir. I'm Professor Edward Cope. The enthusiastic young man beside me is my assistant, Charles Sternberg."

The cowboy accepted the flask and raised it to each of them in a genial toast.

"Charlie. Professor. Good to know you. I'm James Garvey."

⚜

"I knew it. I *knew* you was the cowboy, Garv."

I was so spellbound by the saloonkeeper's story, I jumped at the voice behind me. It was one of the cardplayers, who'd left his game and wandered over to listen. I could see that conversations had quieted at several nearby tables, and others were curious, as well.

"Please, continue Mr. Garvey. Did Professor Cope offer you a job immediately?"

Garvey topped off both of their whiskey glasses.

"Well, not directly."

⚜

Cope was awakened by a jolt, and the frenzied whinnies of all four horses. He shook Sternberg awake.

"What is it?"

"I'm not entirely sure," Cope whispered as he craned his head to peer through the coach's window curtain, "but I think we might be in the process of being robbed."

Outside, four armed men on horseback had surrounded the coach and were forcing the driver to stop. Cope closed the curtain quickly and reached down into the satchel at his feet, producing a small revolver.

"I wouldn't do that if I were you, Professor."

Cope turned to see Garvey holding a six-gun. It was pointed at an ashen-faced Sternberg, who already had his hands raised over his head.

"Well," said Cope, raising his own hands. "This is disappointing."

As Garvey reached out to take Cope's revolver, the stage came to a full stop. Garvey shook his head as he pocketed the smaller gun, looking genuinely apologetic.

"I really hope you don't take this personal, Professor. I don't ordinarily do this sort of thing. I tried being a lawman for a bit, but you can't live on that pay, and work's been scarce . . ."

A gruff shout came from outside the coach. "Garvey! Stop yammering and bring 'em out here!"

"Hold your horses, Stiles!" Garvey shouted back. He sighed regretfully and threw open the coach door. With the barrel of the six-gun, he motioned for Cope, Sternberg, and the preacher to climb out. All three hastened to comply, hands raised, comically stumbling over each other as they climbed out of the coach.

Stiles and another man held shotguns. The other two bandits held pistols.

The stagecoach driver, a wizened little man with a comically large mustache, sat in the driver's box on top of the stage with his hands raised. His eyes widened as Stiles pointed the shotgun in his direction.

"Off the stage, old man!"

"Listen Stiles," said Garvey, "I been talking with these gentlemen—"

"Shut up, Garvey! There's no backing out now."

Garvey shook his head, but kept his six-gun trained

on the passengers. He looked up again as the driver began climbing down from the driver's box, and Garvey caught sight of a metallic glint.

"Wait, he'll kill you!"

But the old man was already raising the small pistol in his shaky hand.

Stiles spun the shotgun around easily and emptied a round into the old man's midsection, throwing him backwards against the stage. The horses reared up, spooked by the shot, and then settled uneasily.

"Thanks for the warning, Garv." Stiles grinned through stained teeth. He spit a wad of tobacco at the old man's lifeless body.

"We said no killin'," Garvey hissed.

"Looks like that plan's been altered."

The other three bandits chuckled at this, exchanging grinning nods. The preacher crossed himself and lowered his head, nervously muttering a prayer for his own life.

Stiles motioned to the other shotgun-wielding bandit.

"Jaffe. Get that strongbox down."

Professor Cope took a step forward. "Please. That's not a strongbox."

"You hold your tongue!" Stiles shouted. "We already killed one. We got nothin' to lose by killin' more!"

Jaffe leaned his shotgun against the stage and began climbing towards the luggage rack on its roof. "Damn straight," he muttered. "Can't be hung but once."

Jaffe was on the roof now, tugging at the straps securing a large wooden box. Cope winced as he tipped it over the edge of the stage and let it tumble to the ground. It splintered and smashed apart, spilling its contents — a pile of fossilized bones—across the dusty road.

Jaffe jumped down and surveyed the wreckage. "Shee-it. There ain't nothin' but old bones here!"

Stiles looked over, but kept his shotgun trained on the passengers. "What? Well, maybe there's something inside of 'em."

Jaffe retrieved his shotgun and began smashing the bones with its stock.

Sternberg and Cope couldn't contain themselves.

"God, no!" shouted Sternberg. "Stop, this instant!" said Cope. He rushed forward and grabbed Jaffe by the arm. Jaffe spun, whacking Cope across the face with the butt of his shotgun.

Cope sprawled backwards into the dust, and Jaffe spun the shotgun around, cocking it. He shoved the barrel into Cope's surprised face. Clearly, he was ready to squeeze the trigger.

Stiles smiled and spit. "Do it," he ordered.

A thin smile crept over Jaffe's face as he drank in Cope's fear. Just as he started to squeeze the shotgun's trigger, the sharp crack of a pistol punctuated the air. Jaffe was thrown backwards, a spray of crimson erupting from his chest. Stiles and the other two bandits froze in place, stunned.

Garvey's smoking pistol spun towards them.

"That's enough! Leave 'em be!"

"You killed Jaffe," said Stiles, in stunned disbelief. "You son of a whore."

Stiles fired his shotgun from his hip as Garvey leapt out of the way and rolled. The shot missed him and tore into the side of the stagecoach. The horses reared up, spooked, and broke into a run, pulling the driverless stage behind them.

Garvey came out of the roll on one knee and lifted his six-gun, firing it in rapid succession with his right hand, while palm-slapping the pistol's hammer with his left. Stiles took all three rounds in the chest and stumbled backwards.

Still on the ground, Cope groped for Jaffe's shotgun. The two remaining bandits opened fire with their pistols, peppering the sand around him. Sternberg broke into a sprint, his bowler flying from his head, and leapt onto one of their backs, hugging the man around the neck and riding him like a bronco. The bandit spun, off-balance, firing wildly.

One of the bandit's rounds caught the preacher in the abdomen. He looked down at the spreading bloodstain in disbelief, and then collapsed.

The remaining bandit's pistol was empty. He tossed it aside, leapt onto his horse, and dug his spurs into the animal's sides, charging wildly at Cope, who was still scrambling in the dust.

Cope struggled to pull the shotgun from beneath Jaffe's lifeless body as the horse thundered towards him, but the weapon wouldn't come lose, and the horse was almost on top of him.

Another pistol-crack filled the air. Garvey snapped off a shot, knocking the rider from his saddle. Cope rolled out of the riderless horse's path just in time, its hooves missing him by inches.

Garvey snapped off a second shot, catching the last remaining bandit in the neck, just before he could put a bullet through Sternberg's forehead.

Cope and Sternberg lay in the dust, bruised and bloodied, each fighting to catch his breath.

Garvey holstered his gun and approached the preacher's lifeless body. He checked for a pulse, and then shook his head, sadly.

Cope stood and brushed himself off. "How did you fall in with these miscreants?"

Garvey sighed. "Bad judgment, I guess. I never thought it'd come to this."

Cope thought on this for a moment. "Good judgment comes from experience, Mr. Garvey. And most experience comes as a result of bad judgment. A smooth sea never made a skillful mariner." He looked to Sternberg, who was attempting to return his crushed bowler cap to something like its original shape. Sternberg looked up, and nodded in solemn agreement.

"As it happens," Cope continued, "we owe you our lives."

"Indeed," Sternberg agreed, placing the sad-looking bowler back on his head.

Garvey looked down at the preacher's lifeless body. "Yeah, well. That ain't gonna bring this preacher back."

"Mr. Garvey . . . may I call you James?"

"Garvey's fine."

"Mr. Garvey—"

"No, just Garvey."

This was simply too informal for the classically educated professor. "Mr. Garvey," he persisted, "every one of us . . . we do what we must, to achieve our ends. That you fell in with these men does not surprise me. What surprised me were the actions you took when their true natures were revealed. Mr. Sternberg and I, we are men of science and civility, but we are also men of common sense. We know that out here, on the frontier, there are unpleasant truths, and even more unpleasant men. You, sir . . . if I may be so bold . . . are a man of action. You have honor, but you also have certain . . . ruthlessness. Those qualities are a commodity to be —"

"Let me save you some time here, Professor. If you're offering me a job, I'll say yes, right off. In fact, consider me an employee, details to be settled over a drink in the saloon we need to find, right after I bury this preacher."

"Yes, of course," said Cope. He glanced down at the preacher's lifeless body. "I was going to add a bit about the preacher. Honoring his sacrifice, and so forth. Making his death mean something . . ."

"Yeah, well . . . let's take that as understood." Garvey got ahold of the man's body, beneath the shoulder blades. "Now, why don't you grab him by the boots, and we'll see if we can find some soft ground by those trees, over yonder."

———————

Garvey lifted the flat rock and hammered the makeshift cross into place at the head of the freshly covered grave. He tossed the rock aside and lifted his hat to wipe the sweat from his brow.

Cope and Sternberg looked on solemnly, their hats in their hands. Garvey caught Cope's eye, and Cope raised an eyebrow, expectantly.

Garvey sighed. "I expect I should say a few words."

"It would seem apropos," said Cope.

Garvey considered for a moment, and then began to speak.

"This here preacher . . . well, there's no doubt he was narrow-minded enough to see through a keyhole with both eyes. That don't mean he deserved this. I expect he believed that when men die, they go to a better place." Garvey frowned. "I'm not so sure about that . . . and I'd soon as not risk finding out for myself . . . but for his sake, I hope that's the case."

Garvey turned around to face a second, nearly identical grave beside the first. "The stage driver . . . well, he made his choice, and paid for it. I heard his nickname was 'Whiskey Jack.' I expect his breath had more than a little to do with that. Whiskey Jack was . . . well, he was a capable driver. Too bad he wasn't a faster draw. May they both rest in peace."

Cope and Sternberg fought off grins and tried to maintain their solemn composures.

"Amen," said Cope.

"Indeed," added Sternberg.

❧

Now, I poured the whiskey, and we'd relocated to a table at the center of the saloon to accommodate the crowd Garvey's tale was beginning to draw.

Outside, the shadows were growing long, and another shift of patrons was arriving, their day's work at some frontier trade ended. Their meager earnings were already earmarked for cards, or liquor, but they were drawn in to the tale like moths to a porch light.

"The stage was wrecked," Garvey was explaining, "but the horses were okay, so at least we weren't on foot, and we had a long ride ahead through rough country."

Behind me a short, rotund woman was catching up a few of the new arrivals in a too-loud voice. Someone else hushed her with an unapologetic "Sssssh!" and she blushed.

"I beg your pardon," she apologized.

Garvey smiled at her kindly, and continued. "By nightfall, we'd made camp, seen to the horses, and made a meal of rations we'd scrounged from the wreck. That night, around the fire, the professor did his best to keep our spirits up by telling us tales about the ancient world, and the strange critters that lived there . . ."

❧

"Millions of years ago," Cope explained, sipping bitter coffee from a dented metal cup, "there was a vast inland sea lapping at the foot of the young Rocky Mountains."

A distant rumble of thunder prompted Sternberg to look up nervously. But Cope seemed not to hear it. He was lost in the distant past.

"This was a different world than our own; a world of strange and forgotten creatures like *Eobasileus* and many others. These creatures may have been lost to time, but their fossilized bones still remain, scattered beneath the plains of the American West. I intend to find them, and study them."

"Before Marsh does," added Sternberg.

Cope scoffed. "Marsh!"

Garvey was rolling a cigarette. "Who's Marsh?"

Sternberg picked up a stick and began poking at the

fire with undisguised contempt. "Professor O. C. Marsh is considered to be one of the leading authorities on extinct forms of life. He's also Professor Cope's greatest rival."

"A 'leading authority,' in this case," said Cope, "appears to be anyone who's guessed correctly more than once. Othniel Marsh is a pompous idiot."

Garvey chuckled at this. "He's got you in a lather, though. That's plain."

"It's impossible to keep up with him," said Cope.

"Marsh has the support of Yale University," Sternberg explained. "He came from a very wealthy family, you see. He even has a wealthy uncle who built a museum for them. Marsh displays his fossils there, which brings great prestige to the university, and in return, they fund his expeditions."

Cope nodded. "Precisely. He's bone hunting in South Dakota as we speak, with a dozen fresh-faced Yalies in tow, no doubt. The student body produces an endless stream of free labor."

The fire began to sputter and pop as droplets of rain began to fall. Cope looked up, frowning. "Marsh spent his whole life being pampered and primped, eating from a silver spoon. He's had every advantage. I doubt he'll last a month in this godforsaken land."

Now the sky opened up and the rain began to fall in torrents. Cope had to raise his voice to be heard above the din.

"I'll wager," he shouted, "that Professor Marsh is pretty miserable about now."

Chapter Two

THE BLACK HILLS, SOUTH DAKOTA

Professor O. C. Marsh sat before an ornate wooden table under a blue sky, sipping tea from a silver service, studying several detailed maps and charts spread out before him. Marsh was impeccably groomed and dressed, and sported a full beard to offset his receding hairline.

"P-pro-professor!" The approaching voice came, between puffs and pants, from Marsh's assistant, a round-faced amiable man in his late thirties. He was red with exertion, and short of breath to the point of wheezing.

Marsh spoke between sips of tea without looking up from his work.

"I'm here, Mudge. What is it?"

Mudge gulped air desperately, trying to catch his breath. "We . . . f-found . . . something . . ."

"Yes? What is it?" Marsh looked up at the sweaty, heaving, overweight man. "What have you found?"

"Eck . . . eck . . . eck . . ."

Marsh tugged a silver flask from his breast pocket and shoved it into the man's shaking hands. Mudge unscrewed the cap and took a large gulp.

"We found . . ." Mudge fell silent as the liquor hit his belly. He looked incredulously at the flask in his hand, engraved with the initials OCM, as though it were the Holy Grail itself. "Good Lord, that's a fine brandy."

"Yes, yes, it's very good. What have you found, Benjamin?"

Mudge was beginning to catch his breath. "Well, I'm not . . . entirely certain. It appears . . . on first examination . . . though I'm by no means an expert on such . . ."

Marsh was losing his patience. "Benjamin, what have you found?!!"

"Well . . . *Equus parvulus*, I think. I'm not entirely certain, but it appears"—Marsh was already on his feet and rushing past him towards the excavation pit— "to be a complete skeleton," he said, finishing his thought to no one in particular. He shrugged, looked down at the flask, licked his lips, and then raised it for another taste. Before it could reach his lips, Marsh reappeared and snatched it from him. "Come on, come on!"

Mudge waddled after him, sighing with disappointment.

———

The path led to a series of earthen ramps cut into the dry, compacted earth. The ramps wound their way to the bottom of a large, recently excavated pit. There, six diggers—all young, fresh-faced Yale students— surrounded a newly unearthed discovery.

One of the students was using a camel-hair brush to sweep debris away from a small skeleton embedded in soil. After a moment, he was able to gingerly disengage a tiny skull from the rest of the bones.

"Clear the way, clear the way."

Marsh reached the bottom of the ramp with Mudge at his heels and approached, his eyes wide with excitement. The student lifted the tiny skull with both hands and carefully handed it to him.

"It's remarkable, isn't it, Professor?"

"Astounding," replied Marsh, his eyes poring over every tiny detail.

The student looked up, noticing movement above at the edge of the pit, and froze. Mudge and several other students followed his gaze, but Marsh was too caught up examining this new discovery to notice their distraction.

"Do you realize what we've found here?" said Marsh. "Why, this is the most pristine example . . ."

He was interrupted by a tap on his shoulder. He turned and saw Mudge looking upward with wide, frightened eyes. Slowly, he turned and followed his gaze.

Surrounding the top of the pit, still on horseback, sat at least a dozen Sioux warriors in full regalia, armed with rifles. Their obvious leader, a remote, majestic figure with red-bronze muscles and a regal countenance, tugged his horse's reins and slowly rode down the earthen ramp into the pit. Marsh, Mudge, and the students remained frozen in place, their mouths agape, until he reached the group and came to a stop.

Marsh swallowed hard, and then opened his mouth to speak.

"Hello" was the best he could manage.

The chief was silent for a moment, considering the odd group before him.

"You dig for gold on sacred land," he said, finally.

"No," Marsh replied, "not gold!"

"The white eye lies!" It was another of the Sioux, a young brave wearing fearsome war paint, shouting from above. Several other braves murmured in agreement, but were silenced when the chief raised his hand.

"We're not looking for gold," Marsh repeated. "Here, look."

Marsh held out the tiny skull. The chief's eyes narrowed.

"What is this animal?"

"A horse."

The chief smiled slightly, and then shouted something to his men in Sioux. They laughed heartily.

"The white eye should stay out of the sun," said the chief.

Marsh couldn't help but become a little defensive.

"Wait. You've seen a horse's bones, haven't you?"

The chief nodded.

"Look at it closely."

Marsh held the tiny skull up alongside the head of Red Cloud's mount, comparing the two. The chief reached down and took the skull gingerly, and peered at it intently, turning it in his enormous but surprisingly dexterous hands.

"A small horse?"

"Precisely," said Marsh, indicated the size with his hands. "Very small."

The other Sioux laughed, but Red Cloud was fascinated.

"Where are these small horses? Show me one."

"I'm sorry, I can't. They are all dead. They died many, many years ago. Many snows. We search for their bones."

"Why?"

"To . . . to honor them. To learn from them."

"They speak to you?"

Marsh smiled. "Oh yes."

"What do they say?"

"They tell us of their world. A world that has long since vanished."

The chief looked down at the skull, then at Marsh. He shouted again to his men, in Sioux, and they lowered their rifles. He dismounted and turned to face Marsh.

"I am Red Cloud."

"My name is Professor Marsh."

"Marsh." Red Cloud tested the name out loud, and then nodded in approval. "I will hear what these small horses have to teach."

———

Red Cloud was born near the forks of the Platte River. His mother, Walks-As-She-Thinks, was an Oglala Lakota, one of the three Lakota bands that made up the Sioux Nation. His father, Lone Man, a Brulé Lakota chief, was raised in the household of his maternal uncle, Chief Smoke.

Lone Man died when Red Cloud was still a boy, and the majority of the chief's early life was spent at war, first against the neighboring Pawnee and Crow, and later against other Oglala.

In 1866, the US Army had begun to construct forts along the Bozeman Trail, which ran through the heart of Lakota territory. As caravans of miners and settlers began to claim the tribe's land, Red Cloud launched a series of assaults on the forts. Thus began the most successful war against the United States ever fought by an Indian nation.

Red Cloud's war was so successful that by 1868 the United States government agreed to sign a remarkable treaty that saw the army abandon its forts along the Bozeman Trail, and granted the land rights to most of western South Dakota, the Black Hills, and much of Montana and Wyoming to the Sioux. This came to be known as the Treaty of Fort Laramie.

Mudge, Red Cloud, and four of the Sioux braves were gathered with Marsh around the small fire pit at the center of the encampment, passing a ceremonial calumet: a long-stemmed peace pipe with a bowl of red pipestone and a festoon of eagle feathers.

The pipe reached Mudge. He accepted it and drew on it eagerly. After a moment he choked and coughed out the bitter smoke, his eyes filling with tears. The Sioux laughed good-naturedly, clapping him on the back.

Red Cloud still held the tiny fossilized skull. It fascinated him.

Marsh produced his brandy flask, twisted off the cap, and held it out to Red Cloud. The chief accepted it cautiously and took a sip. He paused for a moment, considering the taste, and smiled.

"You are different kind of white man, Marsh."

"That is the highest of compliments, Red Cloud. I thank you."

"It is difficult to understand the white man. When the Sioux kill meat, we eat it all up. We do not chop down the trees; we shake down fruits and acorns. We use only dead wood for our fires. The white man—he slaughters the buffalo and leaves him to rot. He plows up the ground. Pulls down the trees. Burns the grass. Kills everything."

Red Cloud took another sip and handed the flask back to Marsh before continuing.

"How can the spirit of the earth love the white man? Everywhere the white man has touched, there is pain." He looked down at the tiny skull, lowering his voice.

"I thought that the white man's Great Father was different. He is not."

Marsh raised an eyebrow. "President Grant is a fine man. It's the men surrounding him that have no character."

"Then he should kill them and find better men. Men like Marsh."

Red Cloud lifted the tiny skull and held it before him.

"The small-horse-whose-world-is-no-more? He is brother to the Indians. Our world is no more. Perhaps we can learn from his mistakes."

———

A short time later, Red Cloud and his men mounted their horses. Marsh, Mudge, and the Yalies prepared to see them off.

"It has been an honor, Chief Red Cloud," said Marsh.

"Marsh. You will speak to your Great Father. Tell him that he has made many promises to my people, and he has broken them. It is better not to make such promises if they will be broken. Will you tell him this?"

Marsh nodded. "I will tell him."

Red Cloud and his party rode off without another word.

Chapter Three

FORT BENTON, MONTANA TERRITORY

Fort Benton's main street was a broad, muddy thoroughfare fronting the western bank of the Missouri River. One side faced docks heaped with barrels, crates, piles of logs and pipes, and other indistinguishable shapes beneath canvas tarps. A rear-paddle-wheel steamboat was moored there, and passengers were boarding. The opposite side of the street was a line of saloons and stores constructed of rough-hewn timber.

Cope, Garvey, and Sternberg arrived on horseback, rain soaked, muddy, and road weary. They moved down the busy avenue passing a traffic jam of Conestoga freight wagons.

Near the side of the road, Cope spied a mangy dog tipping over a trash can, spilling garbage into the street. As he watched, a pig appeared, grabbed a large soup bone in its snout, and ran off with it. The dog barked angrily, and then looked up at Cope with sad, disappointed eyes.

"I know exactly how you feel," Cope told him.

The dog cocked his head curiously, and then resumed rooting through the garbage.

———————

The three men dismounted and tied their horses to a railing in front of a saloon. Sternberg read the faded sign aloud:

"The Occidental Saloon."

"They didn't mean to put up a saloon," Garvey remarked. "Just kinda happened by occident."

Cope smiled. "We've yet to discuss the terms of your employment, Mr. Garvey."

Garvey removed his hat, scooped water from a nearby trough, and slapped it on the back of his neck.

"Well, I'm not exactly swimming in offers right now. What's the going rate for bone hunters?"

Cope rubbed his chin and considered for a moment.

"How does forty dollars a month sound?"

"Sounds reasonable to me."

"Excellent. Let me buy you a drink to seal the deal."

"I wouldn't say no to that."

As they stepped up onto the wooden-plank sidewalk and approached the saloon, the swinging doors burst open and a pile of men tumbled through, arms grappling and punching, legs kicking. Cope, Garvey, and Sternberg sidestepped as the group's forward momentum took them across the sidewalk and sent them tumbling into the muddy street. It was a riot in miniature as five rough-looking cowboys wrestled, punched, and shouted obscenities at one another.

"Spirited town," said Garvey as he returned his hat to his head.

"Indeed," replied Sternberg.

The three brushed themselves off and pushed through the swinging doors into the saloon.

The saloon was huge and bustling with gamblers, river men, cowboys, and prostitutes. Lively music from a banjo player accompanied by a piano wafted across the crowd. Cigars and hand-rolled cigarettes filled the air with smoke.

Cope and company were seated at a table. Garvey had already charmed a pretty young girl, most likely a prostitute. She sat in his lap, whispering in his ear. Sternberg was beaming, enjoying the atmosphere tremendously. He was on the adventure of his young life.

Cope was occupied, interviewing two men: a tall, gaunt scarecrow of a man dressed in buckskin named Jack Deer, and his partner Austin Merrill, a stocky, dark-haired man in a tattered cavalry hat.

"You need a cook and a guide," Deer explained. "Now, I know the Judith River like nobody's business, and Merrill here can cook up any critter that breathes so it tastes like a slice of heaven. That ain't the problem."

"What is the problem?" Cope asked.

"Injuns. Ever since they massa-creed Custer, the Sioux been out-of-control crazy. We'll go, but not for no forty dollars a month. Ain't a man in town'll go for less than a hundred."

Sternberg couldn't contain his shock. "A hundred

dollars? That's preposterous!"

Cope turned to Garvey, who was listening even as the young lady in his lap determinedly nibbled on his earlobe.

"What do you think, Mr. Garvey?"

Garvey lifted the girl from his lap and rushed her off with a wink and a peck on the cheek. He lifted a whiskey bottle from the table and poured for each of them.

"Well now, I been overhearing tads of conversation since we come in here. Seems every third word's been something about Indians. I don't doubt that folks are nervous."

"That's the plain truth," said Merrill.

Garvey continued. "Fact is, we need a guide. And since I'm assuming, on top of my forty dollars, you'll also be feeding me, I'd say we need a cook, too. It's your decision of course. But I say, if you got the means, pay the boys what they're asking. You won't hear no complaint from me."

"All right, then." Cope raised his glass. "Mr. Deer, Mr. Merrill. Welcome aboard. We leave for the Judith River at first light."

Chapter Four

THE BLACK HILLS, SOUTH DAKOTA

The dead man's eyes were wide and glassy. Nearby, a capsized, burned-out carcass of a covered wagon still smoldered. More bodies were strewn about the area—men, women, and children; settlers most likely—their scalps a bloody mess.

Marsh, Mudge, and the Yale students moved through the grisly tableau silently on horseback, staring at the carnage in stunned disbelief.

Mudge pulled up alongside Marsh and spoke in a low voice, so that the students couldn't hear.

"Could this possibly be the work of the Sioux?"

"I won't believe it," said Marsh. "Not this."

Marsh reigned in his horse and stopped. A young woman, barely out of her teens, lay dead before him, her skirt pushed up around her waist.

Behind him, one of the students turned away and

vomited.

Marsh pulled his horse about and addressed the students in a loud, steady voice.

"Gentlemen. This is a terrible sight, and one you'll not easily forget. But, we are Yale men. We must be strong. Mr. Mudge, we will ride to Fort Laramie to report this incident to army officials."

"Yes, Professor."

As they turned the horses and started to head out, a shrieking war cry echoed across the plain.

Marsh reflexively drew his long-barreled Colt Dragoon. Mudge and the others drew smaller pistols.

"Quickly!" Marsh shouted. "Circle the horses!"

In moments, a dozen warriors in fierce-looking war paint rode over the bluff screaming wildly. They thundered towards them brandishing spears, axes, and a few rifles.

Marsh recognized their style of dress immediately. "Miniconjou! They take no prisoners!"

Marsh opened fire, knocking one of the Miniconjou from his mount. Mudge and the Yalies began firing as well, but few were practiced shots.

One of the Miniconjou—their leader, judging by his headdress—fired his rifle and caught one of the students in the chest. He fell from his mount, screaming in pain.

"I'm hit! Oh God, I'm hit!"

Mudge was firing wildly.

"There are too many, Professor!"

"It would seem so," said Marsh, reloading as quickly as he could. "I've enjoyed working with you, Benjamin. You're a fine researcher and a good friend."

Mudge fired again.

"I wish to hell I was a better shot!"

Suddenly the sharp *crack-crack-crack* of rifle shots split the air, and four Miniconjou braves fell from their mounts.

"What in blazes?" Marsh spun and looked behind him. Red Cloud and his party of Sioux galloped towards them, firing their rifles.

Another Miniconjou fell. As Sioux and the Miniconjou rushed towards each other, Marsh and Mudge dragged the wounded student behind a smoldering wagon. The Miniconjou leader spied them, bellowed a fierce war cry, and charged.

Red Cloud circled, sheathed his rifle, and drew a lance. He shouted a Sioux battle cry and lunged into the fray, heading directly for the Miniconjou leader.

The leader saw Red Cloud thundering towards him, raised his rifle, and fired. The round caught Red Cloud's shoulder, tearing into his flesh, but the Sioux Chief didn't flinch or slow. He charged at the Miniconjou leader, lance raised.

The leader let loose a bloodcurdling scream as the lance pierced his chest. Red Cloud tugged the bloody lance from the leader's lifeless body, sending it tumbling into the dust.

With their leader dead, the Miniconjou were demoralized. They retreated, shouting and howling as they vanished over the bluff.

Red Cloud took a moment to catch his breath, and then turned his horse and rode to Marsh's side.

"Your timing is impeccable, my friend."

"Timing," said Red Cloud. "It is the secret to the successful rain dance."

Mudge chuckled at this as he propped the wounded student against the wagon and began carefully checking his injuries.

"You'll be fine, lad. It's not a bad wound."

Marsh looked back to Red Cloud. "Those were Miniconjou, weren't they?"

"From across the White River. Very bad. They would have killed all in your party."

"We are in your debt."

"Their leader was a powerful chief. They will return soon, with many braves. We will not be able to stand against them."

Marsh noticed the blood streaming from Red Cloud's shoulder.

"You're wounded."

"It is nothing," said Red Cloud. "Others riding with me are worse."

"Then let me return the favor. Ride with us. We'll get them medical attention."

"Where?"

Marsh smiled.

Chapter Five

FORT LARAMIE, WYOMING TERRITORY

The sun was setting as Lieutenant T. Emmitt Crawford rushed up the ladder to one of Fort Laramie's open-sided blockhouses. There was another blockhouse over the main entrance and a third on the remaining front corner of the rectangular adobe stockade.

An enlisted man named Appleton was on watch, peering through a set of binoculars at a small dust cloud in the distance, near the river. He lowered the binoculars as Crawford appeared.

"Lieutenant Crawford? You'd better take a look, sir."

Crawford accepted the binoculars and focused them on the scene.

A large party on horseback was fording the North Platte River, heading towards the fort. The two leading horses were being ridden by Marsh and Red Cloud. Mudge and the Yale students were behind them, followed by the rest of the Sioux.

"Christ on a palomino," said Crawford. "That's Red Cloud."

"Yup. And it looks like that old man's got him prisoner."

"More likely, the other way 'round. Go and tell the general."

Appleton rushed down the ladder.

———————

As Marsh and Red Cloud approached the gates, a line of soldiers appeared in the center blockhouse aiming rifles down at them over the rail.

"A welcoming committee," said Marsh. "How thoughtful."

Marsh cupped his hands to amplify his voice and called out to them.

"Please tell your commanding officer that Professor O. C. Marsh of Yale University has arrived. I come with the blessings of Generals Sherman, Sheridan, and Ord."

Lieutenant Crawford's head suddenly popped up from behind the blockhouse rail. He shouted down to Marsh.

"Begging your pardon, sir. Those sure are impressive names you're throwing out, but ain't that Red Cloud you got with you?"

Marsh fought a smile. "Yes sir, it is."

"Well, again, begging your pardon—but could you let us know who's got the upper hand? No offense, but we've had a bit of trouble with him in the past."

"Crawford!" A gravelly voice shouted from inside the fort. "Open the gates!"

"But General, there's a—"

"Now, Crawford."

"Yes, sir."

Crawford nodded to two enlisted men standing down by the gates. They threw the bar and swung them wide, allowing the unlikely party to ride through.

Inside the fort they were met by General John E. Smith, a chiseled and gruff but educated man in his early fifties, with long blond hair and a Custer-style mustache. Lieutenant Crawford rushed over, slightly out of breath, and took his place beside the general. A small crowd of enlisted men began to gather, ogling the scene.

"General," said Marsh, tipping his hat. "I am Professor O. C. Marsh. And this—"

"I know who this is."

The general glared at Red Cloud. Red Cloud stared back, without emotion.

"Red Cloud and his party need medical assistance. We narrowly escaped an attack by the Miniconjou thanks to them."

"You expect me to doctor these Indians with army supplies?"

"I do indeed."

The general scoffed. "Not goddamned likely."

"General," Marsh said matter-of-factly, "under the terms of the 1868 treaty they are entitled to government aid. I'm sure that the Bureau of Indian Affairs in Washington would be most interested . . ."

"All right, all right," said the general. "You made your point. You can bunk them in the stable."

"Is there a source of heat?"

"There's a blacksmith furnace," offered Crawford.

The general's voice dripped with contempt. "Will that be adequate, *Professor*?"

"Perfectly. My men and I will bunk with them."

A murmur went up among the enlisted men. Crawford shushed them and pointed to two men near the front of the group. "You and you. See to the wounded."

The two soldiers nodded and rushed over, heading towards the wounded at the back of the party. The Sioux immediately drew their rifles. Reflexively, the soldiers drew their sidearms.

Red Cloud shouted an order in the Sioux language, and they all froze. There was a moment of tension until Red Cloud broke the silence.

"We will carry our own wounded."

The soldiers nodded, somewhat relieved, and lowered their weapons. They were perfectly content to escort the Sioux to the stables, allowing them to carry their own injured. Redskins made them nervous.

"Will there be anything else?" the general asked, with an unmistakably sarcastic tone.

"Yes, one more thing. My assistant, Mr. Mudge, will be given access to your inventory of supplies and be allowed to draw whatever we might need for the remainder of our journey."

"You haven't the authority!"

Marsh handed the general a folded letter.

"This is an order signed by General Sherman, the head of the US Army, and General Sheridan, who is in charge of the western forts."

Crawford sighed. "That would give 'em the authority, General."

The general glanced at the contents of the order, then pushed it into Crawford's hands and stormed off without another word, glaring angrily at Marsh and Red Cloud.

"Gentleman," Marsh said, turning to Red Cloud and the remainder of the party. "Welcome to Fort Laramie.

Chapter Six

JUDITH RIVER, MONTANA TERRITORY

Cope's party arrived at the Judith River a few hours before sundown. They set up camp and had a fine stew of rabbit, caught by Deer and prepared by Merrill. By the time their meal was finished, night had fallen, and Cope puffed on a pipe of tobacco and read from a tattered Bible by the firelight.

"I never made you for a Bible reader, Professor," Garvey remarked. "You take much stock in it?"

"I was raised among the Quakers. I've outgrown many aspects of organized religion, but I find the Bible to be inspirational, in many respects. There is great power in the poetry of metaphor."

"What part are you reading?"

"A lurid old favorite. The story of Sodom and Gomorrah. The Lord passed divine judgment upon the sinners of Sodom and Gomorrah and they were consumed by fire and brimstone. Then the Lord warned Lot to take his wife and flee from the city, but his wife looked back and was turned into a pillar of salt."

Merrill sat picking his teeth, considering this, and then asked, "What happened to the flea?"

There was a moment's pause, followed by an explosion of laughter, which only added to Merrill's confusion.

Deer playfully tugged his friend's tattered cavalry hat down over his eyes.

"I swear, Merrill. You'd have to study up to be a half-wit."

When the laughter finally subsided, Cope tapped out his pipe, pulled out his tobacco pouch, and began refilling it.

"Do you read, Mr. Garvey?"

Garvey smiled. "My father insisted on it. He could never read himself, and it shamed him. One day he said to me, 'Boy, you got to do something with your life. Why, when Abe Lincoln was your age, he was studying books by the light of the fireplace.'"

"Well, there's no disputing that," said Sternberg. "What did you say?"

"I said, 'Jeez, Paw. When Abe Lincoln was your age, he was President!' He beat the tar out of me for being smart. Next morning he sent me off to school. That seem like a mixed message to you?"

Cope smiled and relit his pipe.

"Your father may not have been a rich man, Mr. Garvey, but your inheritance is priceless. Knowledge is weightless. It's a treasure you can always carry with you."

"Yeah, well. That and two bits won't even get you

a poke in most towns."

———

The following morning, Sternberg was up at first light. He took a bucket down to the river to get water for coffee and to wash up. As he made his way along the bluff near the riverbank, he noticed that his shoe had come untied.

He stooped to tie it, absently whistling a tune he'd heard at the saloon in Fort Benton, when a bullfrog croaked loudly. He turned his head in that direction and noticed something odd about a rock face near the shore. He immediately stood, his untied lace forgotten and dragging behind him, and shuffled towards the spot.

He reached the rock wall, brushed a bit of dirt away with his sleeve and frowned, narrowing his eyes. He brushed a bit more before revealing an odd, raised bump that curved along the wall. He followed it until he reached a hanging tangle of brush that obscured the rest of the wall.

Reaching up, he took hold of the brush and gave it several tugs before it finally snapped and sent him sprawling backwards. He landed on his bottom, sitting in the cold shallows of the river. He leapt up instantly, but his pants were already soaked through. He shook his head and took a breath to utter a string of curses, but they caught in his mouth and he froze.

There, where the brush had been cleared away, embedded in the rock wall, was an enormous, clearly defined fossilized rib cage.

"Professor Cope. Professor Cope!"

He dropped the bucket and ran back over the bluff,

waving his arms frantically. Within moments, Cope and Garvey emerged from their tents and came running.

––––––––––

"It's an entirely new species," said Cope. The skeleton was partially excavated now, and it was enormous. "This one find was worth the price of the entire trip!"

"Damn, it's a big one," said Garvey. "What are you gonna call it?"

"I'll have to examine it further before I decide. It appears to have walked on its hind legs. The forearms are stunted."

Cope leaned in to examine part of the skeleton as Sternberg continued to brush away the siltstone debris that encased it. This caused a small slide of dust, and Cope jumped back with a mouthful of dust. He leaned over, coughed, and spit.

"Blast. My dentures."

"Sorry about that, Professor," said Sternberg.

"Quite all right. Just a bit of grit."

"Dentures?" said Garvey. "You mean fake teeth?"

Cope spit again. "A small piece of bridgework. I'll be right back."

As Cope turned and headed to the riverbank, Garvey looked up at Sternberg.

"You got all your teeth?"

––––––––––

Cope knelt by the river's edge and removed his bridgework. It was a small row of four teeth, but they were in a prominent position. He bent over and rinsed them in the current.

From the opposite bank, among the tall reeds, he heard a rustling sound and looked up. A skinny young Indian, a Crow by the name of Beaver Heart, watched Cope in amazement, his mouth agape.

Cautiously, with one eye on the young Crow, Cope finished rinsing his dentures and put them back in his mouth. Beaver Heart smiled with pleasure, then pointed at Cope and chuckled. He looked around for someone to share his amusement, and then remembered he was alone. He nodded to Cope, smiling, and ran off into the scrub.

Cope stood, brushing off his knees. He glanced back across the river, but the young brave was gone.

"It would appear we have visitors."

Sternberg and Garvey looked up from the excavation as Cope returned.

"Hostiles?" asked Sternberg.

"Hardly."

Garvey pointed to something behind him. "That who you mean?"

Cope turned. Beaver Heart had returned and brought several other Crow Indians with him. One of them appeared to be his wife. Beaver Heart said something to her in Crow, then smiled and pointed at Cope. Cope frowned.

"They seem friendly enough," said Sternberg.

Garvey narrowed his eyes. "What's he pointing at the professor for?"

Beaver Heart grinned, pointed to his teeth, and then

made a motion, as if pulling them out. He pointed to Cope again.

"Oh, I see," said Cope, finally understanding. He reached up and removed his bridgework. Beaver Heart's wife gasped. Cope immediately snapped them back in place. The Crows laughed and clapped, delighted. Beaver Heart tried to remove his own teeth, but failed.

"They think it's a trick, Professor," said Garvey. "They're easily entertained, ain't they?"

Cope laughed, and with an exaggerated flourish, pulled them out again. The Crows nearly fell over, laughing.

––––––––––

Within a few hours, more than a dozen Crow had arrived, and many of them pitched in to help with the excavation, carrying the fossils and stacking them in the buckboard wagon.

Deer, Sternberg, and Garvey watched from a distance as Cope performed his trick for one of the new arrivals.

Garvey shook his head. "Damnedest thing I ever saw. Wasn't a man in town who'd help us out for less than a hundred a month, and here, these're doing it for free, just so long as the professor pops his chompers out every couple of minutes."

"The Crows ain't hard to please," said Deer, "that's for damned certain."

Cope popped his teeth back in, waved to his delighted audience, and returned to the others. "Well, Mr. Deer, we've got more specimens than we can carry. I'd say it's time to head back to Fort Benton."

"You got a wagonful, all right. What'll you do with

all of them, once we get back to town?"

"Take them back to Philadelphia for analysis. I've identified several new species. Professor Marsh could have stumbled onto any one of them. It's crucial that I publish my findings before he does."

"Indeed," said Sternberg.

"Philadelphia?" said Deer. "That's quite a distance. How you planning on getting them all that way?"

"Why, by steamboat, of course."

Deer chuckled heartily. "Well, Mr. Cope. That might be a problem, seeing as how we're five days out, and the last boat of the season leaves in three."

"What?"

"You could probably store them in town, till spring."

"No! That's completely unacceptable! I must publish as soon as possible. There must be some way . . ."

"Lessen you can sprout wings and fly, I don't see past it."

Cope thought for a moment.

"I'll give you and Mr. Merrill a hundred dollar bonus if you get us to that boat before it leaves."

Deer looked up, licking his lips. "A hundred dollars?"

"Each."

"Well, shit. We'll have to ride through the night . . ."

"We can sleep on the wagon, in shifts."

"Well, I ain't promising."

"Your best is all I ask."

Chapter Seven

FORT LARAMIE, WYOMING TERRITORY

General Smith sat in his office holding a hand mirror and grooming his mustache when there was a knock at the door.

"Come."

The door opened a crack, and a very nervous Lieutenant Crawford poked his head into the room. "Begging your pardon, General. This telegraph just came in. It's from General Sherman, sir."

"Well? Come in and read it to me, Lieutenant. Chop-chop."

"Yes, sir."

Crawford entered, closed the door behind him, then cleared his throat and read aloud.

"Sitting Bull and Sioux war party in Montana. Stop. Suspect they are responsible for settlement attacks near Helena. Stop. Fort Benton on full alert. Stop. Arrest

Red Cloud party and await further orders."

A grim smile crept across the general's face.

"So, Sitting Bull has finally done it." He stood and strapped on his sidearm. "Put an armed guard on the Indians immediately. If Marsh gives you any trouble, arrest him, too."

A short time later, Marsh, Mudge, and Red Cloud gathered conspiratorially in a back corner of the stable while a bored armed guard watched them from the door.

"This is unconscionable," whispered Mudge. "Red Cloud's people had nothing to do with the attacks in Montana."

"Sitting Bull," said Red Cloud. "He is a brave warrior, but there is no wisdom in the battles he chooses."

Marsh glanced at the armed guard, who was temporarily distracted by a fiercely determined attempt to extract an uncooperative booger from his own nose. Marsh turned his back to the guard and lowered his own voice to a whisper.

"Benjamin, do you have the inventories I asked for?"

"Certainly." Mudge produced a stack of folded paper from his pocket and passed it to Marsh. Marsh examined them for a moment, and then smiled.

"Excellent. Quite excellent. Can you work a telegraph, Benjamin?"

Mudge looked at him curiously. "What did you have in mind, Professor?"

The young corporal in the telegraph room was sipping coffee from a metal cup when Mudge's head appeared at the door.

"General Smith needs you immediately. He'd like to dictate a telegraph to General Sherman."

The corporal frowned. "Why'd he send you?"

"I was standing beside him when the notion struck," Mudge replied. Then added, "He seems quite angry. I thought it best not to argue."

The corporal jumped so quickly he spilled coffee on some of his papers. "Aw, crimminy!" He frantically tried to sop up the mess with more paper, but gave up quickly when he realized he was making it worse. "I can't do nuthin' right by him, I swear." He grabbed a fresh pencil and pad of paper and rushed past Mudge.

As soon as he was out of sight, Marsh appeared from his hiding place behind the door. He slipped into the room and closed the door behind him.

Marsh tugged the folded inventory sheets from his pocket as Mudge sat down before the telegraph. Unceremoniously cracking his knuckles, he turned to Marsh.

"Whenever you're ready, Professor."

As Marsh began to dictate, Mudge tapped out the message.

"To the commissioner of Indian Affairs, Washington, D.C. . . ."

———

"What?!" The general's booming voice reverberated from behind his office door, followed by the sound of stomping boots crossing the room. The door flew open.

The general emerged, his eyes filled with rage. Crawford followed sheepishly, clutching a crumpled telegraph.

———

"You expect me to let these savages walk right out of here?"

The general stood inside the stables, hands on hips, surrounded by armed soldiers, fuming at Marsh while Mudge and Red Cloud looked on. Crawford stood near the door, looking embarrassed.

"Those are President Grant's orders," said Marsh, calmly.

"Grant! That hack? What lies have you been feeding him?"

"I simply told him the truth," said Marsh. "That the supplies apportioned for distribution to the Sioux, under the terms of the 1868 treaty, have been grossly mismanaged. In many cases, that misuse constitutes fraud. As the bureau liaison for the Red Cloud Agency, you are to be held accountable."

"Lies! All of it!"

Marsh raised an eyebrow. "Lies, you say? He flipped through the folded inventory papers and began to read. "A Mr. J. W. Bosler has a contract for beef at the rate of six and a half cents per pound. The going rate is presently four and a half."

Smith's face was getting redder by the minute.

Marsh continued, "Mr. D. J. McCann has overcharged the government upwards of fifteen thousand dollars for hauling freight. Mr. G. M. Dodge is contracted for corn at the hundredweight price of two dollars and twenty-six cents. The market price is currently one dollar and fifty cents. Would you like me to go on, General?"

The general snatched the papers from Marsh's grasp and shredded them.

Marsh shook his head. "You can't tear up the truth, General. Nor can you twist it to suit your own ends."

The general spoke in a low but unmistakably menacing voice.

"Get the hell out of my fort."

"Gladly." Marsh placed his hat on his head and turned to his companions. "Gentleman?"

They started for the door, but Red Cloud stopped before the general. Without a word, he lifted the general's hat from his head and tried it on. The general was so angry he was shaking, but he didn't move or speak. Crawford looked like he was going to be sick.

"Good hat," said Red Cloud. "Looks better on me."

He headed for the door, still wearing the hat, and one of the armed guards stepped in front of him.

Crawford swallowed hard. "General?"

The general didn't even look up. "Let them go."

———

Outside, the Yale students and the Sioux mounted their horses. As they rode through the gates they were now a single, mixed party, not two separate groups riding together. Marsh, Mudge, and Red Cloud—who was still proudly wearing the general's hat—took the lead as they rode out onto the open plain.

———

After they forded the North Platte River, the two groups separated, preparing to head off in different directions. Red Cloud and Marsh rode away from the group to have a private talk and say their good-byes.

"I asked you to tell your Great Father something," Red Cloud said, "and you promised to do so. I thought you would do what the white man always does and forget your promise. You did not."

He reached down and unlashed something from his saddle. It was the long-stemmed ceremonial calumet that they smoked together in Marsh's encampment the first time they met.

"I think you are the best white man I ever saw. I am honored to call you friend."

He handed Marsh the peace pipe, then tugged the reins of his mount and rode off without another word.

The rest of the Sioux followed, whooping in victory as the Yalies waved and cheered them on.

Chapter Eight

MONTANA TERRITORY

Cope was determined to catch the last steamboat of the season, so the party rode day and night, tugging the bone-filled wagon behind them.

At one point they had to pull the wagon up a steep ridge covered with loose shale. They got thirty feet up the slope before gravity prevailed, and the wagon slipped backwards, toppling the horses. The horses were largely unharmed, but the wagon slid back to the bottom of the ridge. After several disastrous attempts at a direct approach, they used a hastily-constructed windlass — Sternberg was revealed to be quite an engineering aficionado — to pull the wagon up the steep ridge, but they lost at least half of a day in the effort.

The following day the sky opened up. Bolt lightning crackled across the slate-gray sky. They took turns catching fitful naps in the back of the pitching, jostling, rain-drenched wagon. But the party kept driving.

Early the next morning they reached a stream swollen by the previous day's rain. They started across, only to get a wagon wheel lodged in the thick mud of the riverbed.

It was Garvey's suggestion to use all seven of the horses, but Sternberg and Cope devised a harness that maximized the effort.

"Slow and steady, gentlemen. Let the horses do the work. We are guiding their efforts."

Cope was in front, hip deep in water, guiding the horses. Sternberg, Garvey, Deer, and Merrill were each assigned a wheel to guide, to keep the wagon heading in the right direction.

"And . . . forward!"

The reins tightened quickly but evenly as the horses trudged forward. There was a moment's hesitation, but not a loss in momentum, as the wheel broke the suction of the mud and the wagon came free. They all ran with it through the deep water and right up the opposite bank to dry land.

"Excellent! Well done!"

Garvey took a hatful of river water and poured it over his head, smiling in satisfied victory. Just then a row of riders bearing the Stars and Stripes galloped into view over the bluff. Garvey spit and shook his head.

"Well, that's bad timing. The cavalry finally arrives, and we're all done needing saving."

The soldiers approached in an orderly line. The young captain in the lead politely addressed the group.

"Good afternoon, sirs. Might one of you be in charge?"

"That would be me," said Cope.

"Ah. Well sir, I have some . . . travel advice? Sitting

Bull's been spotted less than a hundred miles from here, and heading this way. We've already seen signs of Sioux scouting parties."

"We'll take that under advisement."

"I would, if you value your scalps." The captain paused for a moment, and then dropped his voice and became considerably less official.

"Um . . . can I ask you something, sir?"

"Certainly."

"Well, we've been hearing stories about this scientist-adventurer fella? Goes all around the country, even into Indian territory, getting into danger and risking his life, all to find these bones from giant reptiles? And well, sir—I have to ask. Are you him?"

Cope blushed. "Why, yes. Yes, I am."

The captain grabbed Cope's hand and pumped it vigorously. "Well, it is such an honor to meet you, Professor Marsh!"

Sternberg couldn't help himself. It was as involuntary as a sneeze. He began to laugh, and then laugh harder. It was infectious. They all started to laugh, even the soldiers who had no idea what was so funny.

Everybody except Cope.

———

As the captain's unit moved on, Cope was not in a pleasant mood, and things immediately went from bad to worse. Deer dismounted and began tugging his bedroll and other belongings from the wagon and strapping them to his horse. "Time to go, Merrill."

"What do you think you're doing?" Cope asked.

"You heard the captain. I don't much like the idea of tangling with no Sioux war party."

"He said they were a hundred miles away."

Deer spit tobacco again and pushed his hat back on his head. "No, he said 'less than a hundred miles.' He also said there were scouts already here. I'd imagine they're just as apt to grab a few scalps as old Sittin' Bull." He turned to Merrill. "You coming?"

"I reckon I'm with you, Jack."

Merrill climbed down from his horse to gather his own gear.

Deer nodded in approval, then turned to Garvey and Sternberg. "I'd advise you boys to leave those bones behind and follow along."

"I most certainly will not," said Cope.

"Didn't think you would, but that's your own look out, Professor." He turned to Sternberg and Garvey. "How about you two?"

Garvey remained mounted. "I signed on with the professor. Reckon I'll finish the job."

Sternberg didn't hesitate. "I'm staying as well."

Deer shook his head. "I admire your loyalty, but I think you're crazy as popcorn on a hot skillet. Let's go, Merrill."

The two men mounted up and rode off.

"We best get moving," said Garvey. "That boat ain't gonna wait for us."

———

When the wagon finally topped the rise and it came into view, they all spontaneously whistled, and Garvey said, "Ain't that a pretty sight?"

Below them lay the wide, blue waters of the Missouri River.

"That's the Missouri, or I'm a fool," said Garvey. "The steamer should be able to come upriver this far. We can load the bones and be on our way."

———————

It was nearly dark by the time they reached the riverbank.

"Mr. Garvey," said Cope. "Stay with the wagon. Mr. Sternberg and I will ride to Fort Benton, secure the steamship, and lead them here."

"You know where you're going?"

———————

They didn't. Not entirely. Cope and Sternberg followed the riverbank through the dark woods as best they could on horseback.

Cope squinted into the shadows ahead. "I can't see a damnable thi—"

He was cut short by a low-hanging branch that coldcocked him and knocked him from his saddle. This spooked his horse, and it galloped off into the brush.

"Professor Cope!" shouted Sternberg. "Have you injured yourself, sir?"

"Only my pride, I think. But it's had so many lumps recently, I'm sure it will persevere." He began to stand, then fell back, shouting in pain. "My ankle, it would seem, has a different opinion."

———————

The sun was starting to seep into the gray of the morning as Sternberg led his horse through thick woods and bramble in a vain attempt to keep the river in sight. Cope was slumped in the horse's saddle, his ankle hastily and crudely wrapped with torn bits of cloth. Both men had already stretched the limits of exhaustion, and were rapidly entering the realm of delirium.

"Is it much further, Charles?"

"I'll be honest, Professor. I've no idea."

"Lost then, are we?"

"Utterly. I can't even hear the river anymore. I'm so sorry."

"You've done your best under extraordinary circumstances, old friend. The sun is rising. Perhaps we should resign ourselves —"

A jarring shriek broke the stillness of the morning.

"Do I hear a train?" asked Cope.

Sternberg frowned. "Not a train, I don't think. Sounds like . . ." He fell into silent shock as the realization hit him, then broke into a run, pulling the horse through the brush and bramble until it broke through the tree line.

Chapter Nine

FORT BENTON, MONTANA TERRITORY

The bustling, muddy, rambunctious port was a welcomed sight. The whistle blew again, and they followed the sound to a gleaming red-and-white lacquered steamboat waiting at the docks.

"The *Josephine*," said Cope. She's beautiful, isn't she?"

Sternberg sighed. "Yes, she is."

Captain Princeton W. Grant was a coarse, insolent-looking man with a dark beard and bushy, animated eyebrows. He looked a little put out by Cope's intrusion — he and Sternberg stormed up the gangplank demanding to see the captain — so he was brusque and all business.

"We leave tomorrow morning at nine o'clock, on the button."

"Please, Captain," Cope explained. "My name is

Professor Cope, and I'm a scientist from Philadelphia. We have a four-horse wagon at the steamboat snubbing post three miles upriver. Our baggage and freight are there, and we must take passage for Omaha."

"Well, I'm P. W. Grant, captain of this boat, and if you want to go downriver, you'll have your baggage, freight, and self at this landing at nine o'clock tomorrow morning, when I leave for downriver points."

Cope reached into his pocket and produced a small roll of bills.

"Captain Grant. Surely we can come to some sort of—"

"Son, the Sioux are swarming all over Montana like flies on buffalo shit. You could give me all the money in Philadelphia, plus a dollar. I still wouldn't risk the *Josephine* by making an unscheduled stop."

"Captain, please . . ."

"I'm done talking. I have actual business to attend to. Good day, sir."

The captain turned and headed up a narrow stair to an upper deck.

"Damn him," Cope muttered.

"Perhaps this is the time to resign ourselves to failure," said Sternberg.

"No. There's still time. There must be a way."

———

The young man whistled absently as he strolled down the dock, a fishing pole slung over one shoulder. He arrived at a particular mooring, grabbed a rope attached to the dock, and began pulling it in. In seconds the end of the rope appeared with nothing attached to it. It had been cut. He stared at the frayed end for a moment, incredulous, when he heard a distant voice call out.

"Terribly sorry!"

He looked up in time to see Cope and Sternberg in his rowboat. Cope was aft, yelling through cupped hands. Sternberg was rowing frantically.

"We'll have it back by nine o'clock tomorrow morning, I give you my word!"

The young man tugged an oversized pistol from his belt, lifted it, and fired. The bullet struck the surface of the river a few feet from the boat, splashing Cope in the face.

Sternberg began to row faster.

"I think he might be cross with us."

Another shot ricocheted off the side of the boat, chipping the wood.

"To say the least," said Cope. "Row, Charles, row!"

————————

The three mile stretch upriver seemed endless. Cope and Sternberg alternated rowing duties, and were forced to skirt large sections of whitewater while moving upstream. They were both exhausted by the time they got to the snubbing post where Garvey waited with the wagon.

They took a quick break before beginning the task of transferring all of the fossils from the wagon to the boat. By the time Garvey knotted the final rope, securing the tarp over the bones, it was almost dusk.

Garvey stepped back and looked at the boat.

"I don't know about this."

The weight of all the fossilized bones caused the tiny boat to sit ridiculously low in the water.

"We'll make it," said Cope. "We haven't come this far to fail now."

———————

They were barely a mile downriver and it was already pitch-black. Cope sat at the front of the boat holding a lantern. Garvey and Sternberg each had an oar, and they were doing their best to keep the boat steady, since all three men were precariously perched atop the pile of fossils.

Cope raised the lantern and peered ahead. "There looks to be white water ahead, on the right."

Garvey pushed his oar into the riverbed, gondolier-style, and shouted to Sternberg. "Pull her left, Charlie!"

The two of them struggled with the oars, using them as rudders, to cut a hard left around a white-water eddy. They managed to skirt the first eddy, but the boat was picking up speed.

"More white water to the right!" yelled Cope.

Sternberg lifted his oar to make an adjustment when he heard a loud *thunk* and looked down. The shaft of an arrow had appeared out of the darkness and imbedded itself in the wooden oar.

Sternberg could barely speak, but managed to squeak a single word.

"Indians!"

"Douse the light!" shouted Garvey.

Cope snuffed out the lantern and dropped low, trying to use the mound of fossils as cover. Arrows continue to whip past them. Occasionally one struck the boat, but most fell short.

Garvey snapped off a pistol shot into the darkness, then looked ahead at the raging rapids they were heading into. He could do nothing but shrug.

"Nothing for it. Can't be helped!"

"Got to be the damned Sioux!" said Cope. "We're moving out of their range, at least."

"Hold on!" yelled Garvey as the boat rose, then plunged, surging into the eddy, sending them off on a wild, pitched, white-water thrill ride into darkness.

The three men held on desperately as water surged over and past them. Sternberg lost his grip and began to slip off the side, but Garvey caught him by the collar and pulled him, sputtering, back onto the top-heavy boat.

Another rush of water propelled them forward through a dizzying series of twists and turns before unceremoniously spitting them out the other end into calmer waters.

The three men lay atop the intact pile of fossils, drenched, exhausted, and gasping for air.

Now, Sternberg began to chuckle. Cope and Garvey joined him as it turned into a laugh, and then a belly laugh.

They were going to make it after all.

———————

By sunrise, the deck of the *Josephine* was already bustling with passengers, many anxious to leave town before the impending arrival of the Sioux.

Captain P. W. Grant paced the deck, opening his

pocket watch and checking the time every few minutes. Finally he closed the watch and turned to a nearby member of the crew.

"It's nearly nine. All this Sitting Bull talk is making me jumpy. Let's get going."

"Right away, Captain."

The crewman began to shout orders when he was distracted by the distinct sound of gunshots echoing across the river. A female passenger screamed, others shouted in panic.

"What is it?" shouted the captain. "Is it Sitting Bull?"

"No sir," replied the crewman, pointing upriver. "I believe it's a rowboat."

The captain turned and saw the overloaded rowboat making the last bend with Cope, Sternberg, and Garvey perched ludicrously on top of the fossils. Cope and Sternberg were waving frantically while Garvey fired several more shots into the air.

"Well, I'll be damned," said the captain.

———————

Garvey and Sternberg rushed to get the last of the fossils on board while Cope counted bills into the purser's open palm. "That should cover our passage."

The purser held out a printed receipt. "I'll just need you to sign for the freight."

Cope scribbled his name. The purser nodded in thanks, then squinted at the signature.

"Wait, Edward Cope? Professor Edward Cope?"

"Yes, that's me."

The purser reached into his jacket pocket and produced

a folded slip of paper.

"This telegraph came for you, sir."

"A telegraph? Really?"

Cope accepted the telegraph and began to read as he wandered towards Garvey and Sternberg. They turned, puzzled at the shocked expression on his face.

"Bad news, Professor?" asked Sternberg.

"On the contrary," said Cope. "It's from Washington, D.C. I've been named chief paleontologist of the US Geological and Geographical Survey of the Territories."

"That sounds mighty impressive," said Garvey. "How's it pay?"

"There's no pay at all."

"They'll help finance our next expedition, surely?" said Sternberg.

"I'm afraid not."

"Well," said Garvey, "aside from the fancy title, seems like it don't amount to much."

"You don't understand," said Cope. "I'm now a government official."

"What's that mean?" asked Garvey.

"It means that our next expedition will be sanctioned. We'll have military aid and protection. We'll be able to draw rations and supplies from army posts. Best of all, we'll have access to all the latest government survey maps and geological studies."

Sternberg suddenly understood. "That means . . ."

Cope finished the thought for him. "It means we'll finally be able to compete with Professor Othniel C. Marsh!"

"Now hold on, Garv. I came in late."

It was a local shopkeeper named Earl. Word of Garvey's storytelling was spreading, and one by one, all the residents of Tin Cup were gathering in the saloon to listen. "What's the big deal about this Marsh fellah?" Earl asked. "Seems to me there were plenty of bones to go around. What made Cope so itchy to one-up him?"

"That's a damned good question," I said. "Why were they so competitive?"

Garvey smiled. "It wasn't just about finding bones. It was identifying new kinds of animals that nobody knew about before. The man that finds a new one gets to give it a name. See, in the scientific community, reputations are built on that. How many of these dead animals you give a name to."

Garvey pulled out his pouch and began sprinkling tobacco into the folds of another cigarette paper. The crowd fell silent, recognizing that this action signaled the beginning of a new and interesting chapter of the story.

He twisted the cigarette into shape, caught it in his lip, and struck a match. He lit the cigarette and took a draw before continuing.

"But it goes back further than that for Cope and Marsh. They had bad blood between them from way back. It's a funny thing, but the two men started out as friends. Things turned sour back in 1869, in Philadelphia."

Chapter Ten

PHILADELPHIA, PENNSYLVANIA

His beard was a little less gray and his face a little less creased when Professor Othniel C. Marsh strolled down the tree-lined street of cobblestone, past neat brick townhouses trimmed in marble and glass. A fellow academician, Professor Joseph Leidy, was telling him about one of his students.

"He's brash, but quite brilliant, young Edward. Perhaps my finest student."

"Edward Cope? Yes, of course. We met in Berlin, six years ago. I quite liked him. Twenty-three and taking Europe by storm. We've kept in touch. Did you know I named a species after him?"

"*Mosasaurus copeanus*. An intentional jibe, O. C.?"

"Jibe?" said Marsh, innocently. "How do you mean?"

"Please. *Copeanus*? Cope-anus?"

Marsh smiled.

"It never struck me."

"I'm quite surprised *he* didn't strike you."

"Joseph, please. I consider Edward Cope to be a valued friend and colleague."

They approached a large, vine-covered building bearing a sign:

THE ACADEMY OF NATURAL SCIENCES

Marsh was shocked to see a large crowd gathered outside, many of them members of the press.

"Good gracious. It's a regular circus. What is this great discovery?"

"Only the largest paleontological undertaking of Edward's young career. He's pieced together the bones of a reptilian sea serpent that lived in the waters that covered Kansas one hundred million years ago."

"Kansas? Really?"

The two men pushed through the crowd and entered the building.

————

An even larger crowd was gathered inside in the high-vaulted main gallery. Cope, just twenty-nine years of age and beaming with pride, stood before an enormous shape covered by a tarp. He waved excitedly when he spotted Leidy and Marsh approaching.

"Professor Leidy! Professor Marsh! I'm so honored you could make it!"

"I wouldn't have missed it, Edward."

"Nor would I," said Marsh, reaching out to shake Cope's hand. "Professor Leidy tells me the specimen is from Kansas. However did you get your hands on it?"

"It was sent to the academy by an army surgeon from Fort Wallace."

"Well, I'm anxious to see it!"

"And I am anxious to unveil it!" Cope turned to the crowd and raised his voice. "Ladies and gentleman. May I have your attention?" The buzz of the crowd was reduced to a murmur as Cope prepared to release the counterweights that would lift the tarp and reveal the skeleton.

"Ladies and gentleman," Cope continued, "The Academy of Natural Sciences is proud to present my latest discovery, a wonder of the prehistoric world, the marine saurian *Elasmosaurus platyurus*!"

He released the counterweight and the tarp rose dramatically. The crowd gasped and broke into enthusiastic applause.

The skeleton was nearly forty feet long, with a long snakelike vertebrae that had a neck as long as its tail. Four large fins were attached to platelike hips and chest bones. It had a small angular head with razor-sharp teeth.

"Bravo, Edward!" said Professor Leidy, clapping and smiling proudly at his student. "Just remarkable!"

Cope was grinning from ear to ear.

Marsh was smiling, too. "Quite remarkable, Edward. Truly."

Now Marsh approached the skeleton and began to walk its length, examining it slowly and thoughtfully. He stopped for a moment, rubbing his beard, and then looked up at the razor-sharp teeth in the creature's skull. His eyes narrowed, and he leaned in for a closer look.

Frowning, he glanced back at the tail, then again to the head.

Now, his smile widened.

"Quite remarkable," he repeated.

Cope was thrilled, and turned once again to the crowd.

"Ladies and gentleman of the press, this is my esteemed colleague, Professor O. C. Marsh, one of the world's leading authorities in paleontology."

Marsh bowed. "You are too kind, Edward."

"So," said Cope, loudly. "Tell us what you think of my reconstruction, Professor."

"You've done a remarkable job," said Marsh. "This was certainly quite an intricate puzzle."

"Thank you, Professor," said Cope, beaming.

"However . . ."

Cope frowned. "However?"

"No," said Marsh. "It's nothing."

"Please, Professor. If you have a criticism . . ."

Marsh looked up at the crowd. They had all fallen silent, and the members of the press stood with ears perked and pencils ready.

"Well," said Marsh, "I could be wrong." He paused for dramatic effect. "It's the vertebrae."

"Come again?" said Cope.

"The vertebrae. They seem to be . . . reversed."

Cope turned and looked at the skeleton, nonplussed.

"Nonsense."

Now Professor Leidy stepped forward and squinted at the creature's backbone.

"Why, yes. O. C., I believe you're right."

A low murmur began to travel through the crowd. Cope looked panicked.

"Right? Right? Right about what?" he stammered.

"I believe you've got the whole thing wrong-end most." Marsh pointed to the animal's tail. "That isn't the tail, it's the neck. Simply put, my dear Edward, you've got this creature's head upon its ass."

The crowd burst into spontaneous laughter and finally applause. Cope's face was beet red. Marsh was smiling. Leidy simply looked embarrassed.

※

"If I was to pick a moment when their rivalry truly began," Garvey explained, "that'd most likely be it. The press had a field day with the whole thing. Took years for Professor Cope to overcome that humiliation."

I was furiously scribbling in my notebook.

"So, what about Como Bluff?" I asked, anxious to hear more.

"Now, slow down," said Garvey. "I'm gettin' there. Como Bluff's just where it came to a head, but the real feuding began way before that. It started in Kansas, the following spring. By that I mean the year *after* Marsh befriended Red Cloud and Cope stole the rowboat."

"Sorry, Mr. Garvey," I said. "Please. Continue."

"Well, that was the start of a new collecting season. Cope and Marsh were back east all winter, publishing papers and naming dead animals. Now, the time had come for more bone hunting."

Chapter Eleven

THE KANSAS-PACIFIC RAILROAD

The Pullman car was lavish, sporting curtained sleeping berths and several sitting-room areas with polished wood interiors and velvet drapes.

Marsh and Mudge were seated in one of these areas across from a vigorous, elfin gentleman with a receding hairline of black curls. They were all smoking cigars.

"Say, have you heard this one?" asked the curly-haired gentleman. "A man walks into a bar room with a lion. He asks the bartender, 'Do you serve politicians here?' The bartender says, 'Sure I do.' The man says, 'Okay. Give me a whiskey and a politician for the lion.'"

Marsh smiled politely but didn't laugh. Mudge just looked confused.

"That's a very funny joke. I must assume you've heard it. That, or you're a politician yourself."

Marsh shook his head. "No, I'm not a politician."

"Well if you don't mind my asking, what do you do, sir?"

"I'm a scientist."

"Really?" said the curly-haired man, suddenly curious. "The earth sciences?"

"That's right."

"I'm a big fan of the earth sciences."

Mudge couldn't help but interject. "You're the showman, aren't you? P. T. Barnum?"

"That's me."

"I saw your show once," said Mudge, smiling. "In New York."

"What did you think?"

"It was . . . diverting."

"Diverting?" said Barnum, raising his eyebrows.

Mudge shifted in his seat, uncomfortably. "Well, if you don't mind my saying, most of it seemed like humbug and fakery."

"Ha!" Barnum laughed. "Of course! P. T. Barnum's Grand Traveling Museum, Menagerie, Caravan, and Circus is the greatest show of humbug and fakery on earth! I give my audience entertainment. Mysteries and miracles galore. I'm not in the truth business."

"I see," said Marsh. "As Pushkin, the Russian poet once said, 'Better the illusions that exalt us than ten thousand truths.'"

Barnum pointed at Marsh, nodding in agreement. "That's the ticket, exactly!"

"I suppose entertainment has its value," said Mudge.

Barnum tapped the ash from his cigar into a brass

receptacle. "So, you're in the earth sciences, are you? I'm a bit of a collector myself. This should interest you. I recently purchased some remarkable pre-Columbian relics in Mexico. They should have made me a fortune."

"Should have?" asked Marsh.

"I shipped them to New York. My agent had no idea of their value. The idiot put them up for sale."

"And they were sold?"

"Oh, yes. Some little cuss up in New Haven bought them."

"I thought as much." Marsh reached into his jacket pocket and produced a business card.

"What's this?" said Barnum, accepting the card.

"I'm the little cuss from New Haven."

Barnum stared at the card in stunned silence, looked up at Marsh, then burst into fits of laughter.

"That's perfect. You're the little cuss. Priceless!" Barnum reached into a leather satchel at his feet and produced a bottle of cognac. "You must have a drink with me!"

Chapter Twelve

HAYS CITY, KANSAS

Hays City was a bustling railroad town. The tracks of the Kansas-Pacific ran right down the middle of Main Street between a varied and colorful collection of shops, saloons, and bordellos, and business was always brisk. But the rough-and-tumble metropolis really came alive after sunset, when tinny piano music, distant gunfire, and wild laughter began to echo through the lamplit streets.

Barnum, Marsh, and Mudge entered Tommy Drum's Saloon shortly after dusk, pushed their way through the raucous crowd, and approached the bar. The saloonkeeper recognized Marsh immediately.

"Why, if it isn't the bone professor himself!"

"It's been a few years, Tommy. I'm honored that you remember me."

"All part of the job, sir."

"This is my assistant, Benjamin Mudge. And this

. . ." said Marsh, with an exaggerated flourish, "is the renowned showman P. T. Barnum. Gentleman, meet Tommy Drum."

Tommy's face lit up. "P. T. Barnum in my saloon? No horseshit?"

"In the flesh," said Barnum, extending his hand. "A pleasure, Mr. Drum."

"Well, let me set 'em up for you gents, on the house!"

As Tommy poured, Marsh surveyed the room. The crowd was loud, colorful, and animated, but his eyes were immediately drawn to a particular table, where a striking young woman with a mane of red curls was shuffling cards. A small crowd had gathered around her.

"Tommy," asked Marsh. "Who is that young woman?

"Pretty lady, ain't she? Name's Rae Callahan."

Seamus and Rae Callahan were among the wave of immigrants from Ireland and other parts of Europe that flocked to America in the late 1870s. They first settled in Chicago, where that city's meatpacking establishments, rail yards, and factories were plentiful and offered many employment opportunities for unskilled laborers. But, manual labor suited neither Seamus nor Rae, and eventually they headed south.

It was Seamus's idea to purchase a wagon, paint it in garish colors, and stock up with a cargo of colored water with fancy labels. He anointed himself "Professor," deciding that his extended tenure with the University of Life qualified him to utilize such a moniker.

Rae was instructed to wear a low-cut gown that

accentuated her bosom while she performed as his dutiful assistant. In between shows, for a small additional fee, she read fortunes with tarot cards.

And thus, their business venture was born:

Professor Callahan's Sorcery Serum

THE GREAT MEDICAL WONDER!

THERE IS NO SORE IT WILL NOT HEAL, NO PAIN IT WILL NOT SUBDUE.

PLEASANT TO TASTE— MAGICAL IN ITS EFFECTS!

Their routine was simple and effective. They would set up their wagon in the center of town at the busiest part of the day when the streets were overcrowded with potential marks, sell off as many bottles of their magical "cure-all" as they could, and then leave town just as quickly, ensuring that they were miles away before their customers began to suspect they'd been had.

Things went quite well for a time, but fate caught up with them in Hays City where, after a particularly lucrative medicine show, Seamus decided he'd like to try his hand at cards before they hit the road again. In his estimation, he could double or even triple their nest egg very quickly in a town with such a well-to-do, open-minded population.

He'd lost all of their money, and was accumulating

a substantial debt, when a drunk cowboy stumbled in off the street waving his guns around and shouting for "that Mick snake oil salesman!"

Seamus was shot dead, the wagon was confiscated by the local law, and Rae found herself stranded in Hays City, depending on her tarot readings to eke out a living.

————————

"Rae come into town a year or so back," Tommy Drum was saying, "with her husband. He was a slick one, hawking medicine show wares."

Barnum raised an eyebrow. "A married woman? Careful, O. C."

"Well, she's a widow now," said Tommy. "Some gunslinger decided his cure-all didn't cure all it promised. Shot him dead. Good riddance, I say. He was a scoundrel of the first order." He hooked a thumb towards her table and lowered his voice a bit. "Course, that one sitting across from her is even worse. That's George Newcomb. They call him the Slaughter Kid."

————————

Newcomb, a sneering, rat-faced gunslinger, was eyeing Rae like a hungry dog eyes a pork chop. His three riding buddies, Troy, Angus, and Getz stood behind him, passing a bottle of whiskey between them.

Rae's green eyes fluttered nervously as she held the deck out to Newcomb.

"Now, if you'd be so kind as to cut the cards?" Her voice had the soft lilt of an Irish accent.

Newcomb smiled leeringly at her and cut the deck.

"I'll wager there's a pretty fortune-teller in my future,"

he said.

"Careful now, Kid," said Troy. "You get a full house with them tarot cards, you might kill us all!"

Newcomb looked up at him. "I might kill one of you just for bein' a pain in my ass."

Angus and Getz thought this was hilarious. Troy just looked nervous.

"Now, Kid. I'm just funnin'."

Newcomb ignored him and turned back to Rae. She laid out a row of three cards, facedown.

———

Marsh and company watched from the bar, fascinated.

"The Slaughter Kid?" Marsh asked, raising a skeptical eyebrow.

"Never heard of him? They also call him 'Bitter Creek Newcomb.' He was a cowhand before he turned to robbin' banks and trains. Rode with the Daltons for a piece, and the Doolin gang? He's probably the most vile son of a bitch in Hays City."

———

At the table, Rae turned over the first tarot card. It showed a skeleton riding a horse, surrounded by dead bodies.

Newcomb's eyes went wide. "That's the death card! You sayin' I'm gonna die?"

"Now, now," said Rae. "There's no need to get yourself worked up. The death card doesn't always mean death."

"Then what's it mean?"

Rae shrugged. "Great change. A major turning point.

Often, it's a very good thing."

She turned the next card. It was a picture of a stone tower being violently struck by lightning.

"That don't look good, neither!" said Newcomb.

Rae shifted uncomfortably in her seat. "Well, it . . . ah . . . generally means . . ."

"It means what?"

"Well . . . catastrophe."

"That's bad, ain't it? Catastrophe's a bad thing!"

Rae swallowed nervously, but didn't reply.

"There's one more card there! Turn it over!"

Rae smiled. "It's just a game, friend. You shouldn't take it so —"

In a blur, Newcomb was standing, pistol drawn, the muzzle pointed at Rae's forehead. She froze, eyes wide. Beneath the table, her manicured hand fumbled for the single shot Derringer she kept tucked in her boot.

"Turn the damn card!" Newcomb shouted.

Marsh couldn't stand it anymore. He jumped to his feet and approached.

"Now, see here!"

The gunslinger spun around, pointing the gun at Marsh.

"You got something to say, old man?"

Now Rae was on her feet, raising the Derringer. Angus, the largest of Newcomb's cohorts, saw the tiny pistol and immediately grabbed her from behind, pinning her arms. The Derringer went off, firing harmlessly into the floorboards.

Newcomb hauled back and struck Marsh across the

forehead. Marsh stumbled back, blood streaming from his forehead. Newcomb turned and pointed his gun in Rae's face. She struggled helplessly as Angus held her arms. Newcomb snatched the empty Derringer from her hand and tossed it on the table.

"Now sit your ass down!"

Angus pushed her back down into the seat.

"Now," Newcomb sneered. "Turn . . . the goddamned . . . *card*!"

With a trembling hand, Rae reached out and turned the final card. It was the Hanged Man.

"Jesus!" whispered Angus.

The color drained from Newcomb's face, and his fearful expression twisted into a scowl. "You did that on purpose!"

Rae shook her head. "No, I—"

"You stacked the deck! You goddamned whoring bitch. You stacked the deck!"

Newcomb cocked his pistol.

From out of nowhere, a hand appeared around Newcomb's wrist. With a single, fluid motion, the wrist was jerked up and back with an ugly *snap*. Newcomb shrieked in pain as his gun tumbled to the floor. He looked up in shock at the man gripping his broken wrist.

"Wild Bill."

The impeccably dressed gunslinger was bigger than life. James Butler Hickok, better known as Wild Bill, had long, sandy-brown hair and an almost comically large mustache. Everybody knew him by reputation, if not by appearance.

"I believe you owe this lady an apology," said Wild Bill.

"I . . . I didn't know you was in town, Bill . . . I . . . I'm sorry, ma'am. I meant no offense."

"That's more like it," said Wild Bill.

Reaching up with his free arm, Wild Bill slammed Newcomb's face down on the tabletop, shattering several glasses and the gunslinger's nose simultaneously. Then he stood him up, spun him around, and ran him headfirst into the bar.

Newcomb fell to the ground, moaning quietly. Wild Bill sauntered over, grabbed Newcomb by the belt, and threw him face-first through the swinging saloon doors into the muddy street. He turned towards Troy, Angus, and Getz.

"You still riding with that skunk?"

"No sir," said Troy without a moment's hesitation, "we are not. And if I may say so, Mr. Hickok, that thrashing you gave ol' George was long overdue."

Wild Bill smiled warmly, then punched Troy square in the nose. He teetered for a moment, then dropped like a sack of wet cement.

"As was that, I do believe."

Angus and Getz were frozen in place, staring at Wild Bill in terror. Wild Bill narrowed his eyes at them. "Boo!"

Angus and Getz stumbled over each other in their mad rush to push through the saloon doors and escape into the night.

Rae was already helping Marsh to his feet and wiping his bloody forehead with a handkerchief.

"That was very valiant of you. And rather foolhardy, Mister . . . ?"

"Professor. Professor O. C. Marsh, at your service,

my dear." He bent over and kissed her hand.

Wild Bill reappeared, grinning and brushing his mustache with thumb and forefinger. "Just like old times. I reckon I missed this town." He shook Marsh's hand. "Appreciate a man who stands up for a lady."

"The gratitude is mine, Mr. Hickok," said Marsh. "Please. Let me buy you a drink."

"Much obliged, sir."

———————

The legend of Wild Bill Hickok had grown over the years, spread by word of mouth and embellished by dime novels. There were many popular stories, but one of the most popular occurred right there in Hays City, in 1869.

James Butler Hickok was younger then, and serving as the town marshal. He was patrolling Main Street when erratic gunfire began to echo from the eastern end of the street. It was a man named Bill Mulvey, a notorious gunslinger from Missouri with a nasty reputation as a cold-blooded killer.

On this particular day, Mulvey was staggeringly drunk. As he reeled back and forth across the street he was randomly firing shots into the various saloons and business establishments, deriving great pleasure from shattering mirrors and bottles of liquor within.

Mulvey was obviously looking for trouble, and when someone told him that Wild Bill was the town marshal, Mulvey swore to find Hickok and to shoot him on sight. As he became drunker and even more belligerent, he even began to profess that shooting the marshal was his entire reason "for coming to this damn town in the first place!"

By the time news of his threats reached Wild Bill, Mulvey was already in view, heading in his direction, rifle in hand. Wild Bill stepped out into the street, and Mulvey slowed, squinting at the figure before him, his vision somewhat impaired by his consumption of alcohol. He began to raise his rifle.

Thinking fast, Wild Bill looked past Mulvey and waved his hand as though he were trying to catch the attention of someone behind him.

"Don't shoot him in the back," Wild Bill called out. "He's drunk!"

Mulvey wheeled around, raising his rifle in the direction of the imaginary man he thought Wild Bill was addressing, and fired wildly. Wild Bill lifted his six-shooter and fired once. Mulvey dropped with a bullet through his head.

"I won't be having drunken idiots shooting up my town," he said, later.

Wild Bill did little to diminish the attention he fostered in the press. One story claimed he killed a bear with his bare hands and a bowie knife. Another told the story of how Hickok had pointed to a letter "O" that was "no bigger than a man's heart," on a sign some fifty yards away. Without sighting his pistol, the story claimed, he fired six shots from the hip, each of them hitting the direct center of the letter.

———

Inside Tommy Drum's Saloon, Wild Bill and Rae Callahan joined Marsh, Barnum, and Mudge at their table and proceeded to buy each other drinks for the next few hours. Before long, Barnum was trying to convince Wild Bill to join his show.

"You're a living legend," said Barnum. "I can make you very rich."

"Thanks, but no thanks, Mr. Barnum. I got no need to be rich. Besides, I spent a little time with Buffalo Bill's show a few years back. I'm afraid I ain't got the right disposition for show business. No, I'm headed back to Deadwood. If I got any friends in this world, I reckon they're all there."

Across the table, Rae was making a show of reading Marsh's palm.

"I see strength and great determination, Professor. Many challenges and many victories. You're to have a long and fruitful life."

Mudge scoffed. "Bah. The professor doesn't believe in . . ."

Marsh, enraptured by Rae's attentions, finished Mudge's sentence. "Having a closed mind about anything."

Mudge shook his head. "There's a first time for everything, I guess."

Marsh ignored him. "What else do you see, my dear?"

She ran her manicured nails over the surface of his hand, lightly. Marsh squirmed a bit in his chair and cleared his throat.

Rae continued. "I see a great rival in your future. A man. A younger man. He's a jealous one. He wants what you have, and he'll fight you tooth and nail to get it."

"Yes, yes! Quite correct. That's remarkable!"

"Do you know who this man is, Professor?" asked Rae.

"I certainly do."

Mudge shook his head. He'd never seen Marsh so distracted, and it worried him. Anxious to change the subject, he turned to Wild Bill.

"Mr. Hickok. How about showing us one of your famous shooting tricks?"

Wild Bill downed another shot of whiskey and smiled.

"Why not?"

He turned to Rae.

"Miss Callahan? Would you have a small mirror handy?"

"Sure and I do, Mr. Hickok."

She released Marsh's hand and reached into her purse, removing a small silver mirror. Wild Bill took it with a smile and a tip of his hat.

"Much obliged, ma'am."

Standing, he grabbed a bar stool and set it near the door, then placed his empty whiskey glass on top of it. The piano fell silent as the crowd murmured with interest. Those near the stool nervously cleared the area.

Wild Bill unholstered his pistol and returned to his seat. He pointed the pistol backwards, over his shoulder, and raised the mirror with his left hand, using it to aim.

"One . . ." he counted, "two . . . three . . ."

When the pistol shot rang out, everybody in the saloon turned to look at the stool. The glass remained where it was, unbroken.

"You missed," said Mudge.

"Not entirely," said Wild Bill.

As if on cue, a figure carrying a rifle stumbled forward through the saloon doors and crumpled to the floor, shot through the heart. It was the gunslinger, George Newcomb.

"Son of a bitch tried to shoot me in the back," said Wild Bill.

Now, without really aiming, Wild Bill casually fired a second shot over his shoulder. The whiskey glass shattered. He tossed the mirror back to Rae.

"Now," said Wild Bill, holstering his pistol and standing, "I believe it's time for another drink." As he headed for the bar, the piano started up again. The crowd apparently took this as a cue to return to their own drinking and gambling. The show was over, and someone was already dragging the body into the street.

As Barnum watched Wild Bill step up to the bar and motion to the bartender, he shook his head in amazement. "I want that man in my show."

"You should hire Miss Callahan," said Marsh.

"I'm afraid palm reading doesn't play under the big top. Now, if she could swallow swords or swing on a trapeze . . ."

Wild Bill returned with a fresh bottle of whiskey and filled everyone's glass. Rae nodded in thanks and downed hers quickly, licking her lips. She was getting a little tipsy.

"I've never seen anything like it," said Marsh. "She was able to tell me all about myself. Things she couldn't possibly know. She even mentioned Cope."

"I can do her one better," said Wild Bill.

"What do you mean?"

Wild Bill closed his eyes, put his fingers to his temples, and hummed loudly in a comic parody of a fortune-teller.

After a few moments he opened his eyes and immediately downed a shot of whiskey.

"The spiritual power of this here whiskey will reveal all," he pronounced dramatically. He looked Marsh in the eyes, his face gravely serious. "This Cope. He's a tall feller. Thirty-five, maybe. Fair haired. Talks up a storm. Travels with a younger feller. His name's . . . Stoneby . . . Stoneberg?"

"Sternberg?"

"That's him! How am I doing?"

Rae smiled at him, blearily and dreamily. "A trick-shooting, mind-reading cowboy, is it? Where can I get my own, I wonder?"

Wild Bill winked and poured more whiskey into Rae's glass and his own.

"I'm speechless," said Marsh. "That's remarkable, Mr. Hickok. What's the trick?"

Rae and Wild Bill toasted each other and downed their whiskey in unison. Wild Bill immediately refilled both glasses.

"No trick," said Wild Bill. "I ran into him, not fifteen miles out of town. Said he was headed for the Saline River."

"What?" shouted Marsh.

"It's a fact."

"Damn him!"

Mudge leaned over and urgently whispered, "The Saline River? He's got a jump on us, Professor. We should leave as soon as possible!"

Marsh shook his head angrily. "How did he know our destination? Where is he getting his information?

Damn him! I wish I had a spy in that camp."

This last remark caught Rae's ear. She leaned over, smiling broadly. "Do you, now?"

"More than anything."

Rae's smile vanished, and she instantly transformed from ingénue to businesswoman.

"Professor Marsh, I don't know if it's obvious, but I don't belong in this town. I'd do anything to get out of it, short of selling my virtue to mule skinners. Every time that train pulls out, I wish I were on it."

"I understand, completely."

"Tell me. This Cope. Your greatest rival, you said. Suppose I were to . . . befriend him for you? Keep an eye on his comings and goings. Find out what he was up to. What would that information be worth to you?"

Marsh smiled in understanding and lifted his glass to her. "Quite a lot, Miss Callahan. Quite a lot."

She raised her own glass and returned his smile.

"I'd say you've found your spy," said Rae, with a wink.

Chapter Thirteen

THE SALINE RIVER, KANSAS

An empty whiskey bottle was balanced on the top of the rock outcropping. A shot rang out, and the bottle vanished in an explosion of glass shards.

Garvey spun his pistol expertly and returned it to his holster with a flourish.

"See? Nothin' to it."

Cope shook his head in awe. Sternberg stood nearby, watching quietly.

"I could never do that," said Cope.

"We been lucky so far, Professor, but if we're gonna spend much time on the frontier, you best learn to protect yourself. All it takes is practice."

"I'm willing to try."

Garvey shouted to another man standing off to one side.

"Lucas. Set up five or six!"

"You got it, Garv," said Lucas. The newly hired digger began removing bottles from a burlap sack and setting them in a row along the top of the ridge.

"You don't got to learn a fancy draw or nothing," Garvey explained. "Just get your shootin' down."

Cope shook his head skeptically, but stepped up to give it a try.

"Aim with two hands. Sight down the barrel, but aim a tad high. Take a breath and hold it in, then squeeze the trigger."

Cope fired, missing completely.

"Not bad for a first," said Garvey. "Don't jerk on the trigger, just squeeze slow and even."

Cope fired again. This time he took a chip out of the rock, inches from one of the bottles.

"That was good."

"Very good," said Sternberg.

Garvey turned. "You gonna try, Charlie?"

Sternberg shrugged. "I already know how to shoot."

Garvey smiled. "Well then, let's see what you got!"

Sternberg looked embarrassed. He turned to Cope. "Professor, I don't think I need to . . ."

"Come on now, Charles," chided Cope. "Be a sport."

"All right."

Sternberg stepped up, unholstered his pistol, and took aim. A bottle shattered with his first shot.

"Charles!" said Cope. "I'm impressed!"

"That was lucky," said Garvey, squinting at the glass shards.

"Lucky?" said Sternberg.

"Well, sure."

Sternberg frowned and returned the pistol to his holster. He took a deep breath then drew it with lightning speed. Five shots rang out in succession. Five bottles shattered. After a moment's pause, Sternberg spun the pistol with an intricate flourish and returned it to his holster.

"Woo-hoo!" shouted Lucas. "Hot damn!"

Sternberg turned to Garvey, whose mouth was agape. "I guess it's my lucky day," he told him.

A clanging bell sounded in the distance.

"That's for me," said Sternberg. "I'm needed at the quarry. But thank you for the, ah . . . lesson." He smiled and jogged off. Garvey watched him go, shaking his head in amazement.

"I'll be goddamned."

"Charles was raised right here in Kansas," said Cope, as though that would explain it.

They both turned their heads at the sound of Lucas's wolf whistle. A horse was emerging from over the bluff, and its rider was a pretty young woman in a dress, riding sidesaddle. She smiled pleasantly as she approached.

"I hope you'll forgive me for being a disturbance, gentleman," she said with an Irish brogue that was almost musical.

"Disturb away, ma'am!" said Lucas.

"Well, I fear I've got a bit turned around. Am I a fair way from Hays City?"

"Quite a distance, I'm afraid," said Cope.

"Oh, for the love of God," said Rae, starting to dismount. "I'm only after a long day's ride in the sun, and now I find I've just as long a ride before me to get back to town?"

Cope rushed over to help her down. As she landed on her feet she held up for a moment, and she and Cope were nose to nose, his arms on hers. He looked at her green eyes, speechless and captivated.

"A gentleman, is it?" she said, smiling at him. "Why, you're as rare as hen's teeth in these godforsaken lands. I'm Rae Callahan. And who might you be?"

"Edward. Edward Cope."

"A fine name for a fine gentleman."

Garvey cleared his throat loudly. "Fine, fine. We're all fine. Thanks for asking."

Suddenly conscious of Rae's proximity, Cope pulled away, embarrassed.

Garvey squinted at Rae against the sunlight. "You been riding by yourself all that way, huh?"

"Irish women are shockingly independent. A character flaw I suppose."

"I suppose," said Garvey.

She glared at Garvey for a moment, and then turned back to Cope, smiling sweetly.

"Well, I'm fairly knackered so I should be heading back to town if I'm to make it by dusk. Could you point me in the right direction?"

"Nonsense! One of my men will escort you," Cope insisted.

"Here it comes," Garvey muttered to himself.

"Mr. Garvey, would you see that Miss Callahan gets safely back to Hays City?"

"Well, I don't wish to be a fret . . ." said Rae.

"Heavens, no. Mr. Garvey doesn't mind. Do you, Mr. Garvey?"

"Mind? I got no mind. I couldn't pour water out of a boot if it had instructions on the heel."

"Well," said Rae, "then I'm the lucky one to be fallin' in with such fine, fine gentlemen. But do you mind my asking what in Janey Mac you're doing out here in the middle of nowhere to begin with?"

"Professor!" It was Sternberg shouting from the quarry. "Professor! Come quickly!"

Cope smiled and offered Rae his arm. "Miss Callahan, allow me to show you exactly what in 'Janey Mac' we are doing."

———

The "quarry" was a large excavation pit with wooden ramps and scaffolding. The floor was laid out in a grid of string tied to short posts. Sternberg and several more of the locally hired diggers stood inside a grid square near the back wall.

As Cope, Rae, and Garvey approached, the diggers stepped aside to let them see the discovery—the partially excavated skeleton of an impossibly huge winged creature.

"Fantastic!" said Cope.

Rae couldn't believe her eyes. "Jaysis, Mary, and Joseph! A dragon, is it?"

Cope smiled. "No need to call Saint Peter. It's a pterodactyl. They were huge reptiles that flew through prehistoric skies on leathery wings."

"Right. Well . . . can you be sure it didn't breath fire?"

"Well, I suppose I can't be *sure* . . ."

"Well, then. Call it what you like, but it looks like a dragon to me."

Garvey chuckled at this.

Sternberg couldn't contain his enthusiasm. "Look at the size of it, Edward. The wing span must be in excess of twenty feet!"

"Yes, this is undoubtedly a new species. Professor Marsh will be green with envy!"

"Professor Marsh?" said Rae. "Professor O. C. Marsh?"

"Yes. Why? Do you know O. C. Marsh?"

"Why, I met him only yesterday, at Tommy Drum's place. He was with P. T. Barnum and Wild Bill Hickok."

Cope was nonplussed. "P. T. Barnum and Wild Bill . . . ?"

"Hickok."

"But that's absurd!"

"That it was. It was quite a memorable night."

"I'll bet it was," muttered Garvey.

Rae ignored him. "Funny," she said to Cope. "Marsh looked like a ghost when someone mentioned your name as well. I'm curious, Mr. Cope. Why this row between the two of you? What's that all about, now?"

"Marsh." Cope grimaced. "Marsh is a . . . a rival. And a cheater. Perhaps even a thief. Certainly a bully. He's the worst kind of scientist. Unprincipled, inaccurate, dishonest. He gives our profession a bad name."

"Right, well. He does sound horrible."

Cope looked up at her, his mind suddenly filled with questions.

"Did he mention where he's heading? Where he's planning to dig? Did he mention anything?"

"I'm afraid not. Or perhaps I wasn't listening," said Rae. "But, here's a thought. What do you think you'd give to stay a jump ahead of him?"

"Anything!"

Rae smiled. "Ah. Well, I was thinking more of a specific dollar amount. I'm curious, hypothetically, what that kind of information would be worth to you?"

Cope smiled and reached into his jacket for his book of bank checks.

Garvey did as Cope asked and set out with Rae on horseback to escort her to Hays City. It was still early afternoon, so they took a leisurely pace and rode in silence for nearly an hour. Eventually Rae couldn't stand it and pulled her horse alongside his, matching his pace.

"So," she said, trying to make conversation. "Working with scientists, digging up dragon bones? Your mother must be very proud, Mr. Garvey."

"How's yours feel about you being a spy?"

She frowned. "If you've something on your mind, out with it."

"I saw Professor Cope give you that money."

"I believe I saw him write you a check as well."

"I earned that. That was my regular pay."

"And I hope this was the first of mine."

He had no reply to that.

"Why don't you like me?" she asked.

"Cope gave you that money to spy on Marsh."

"So?"

"I don't trust spies."

"Fair enough," said Rae. "But let me ask you this. Do you *like* me?"

Garvey sighed. "Well, yeah. I suppose I like you just fine."

"Then that'll have to be enough for the time being, won't it? Tell you what? We'll work on trust, right after I teach you how to pour water out of a boot."

Garvey chuckled.

Rae glanced around at the harsh desert landscape. "It must be a hard life out here, Mr. Garvey. I wonder, don't you ever see yourself in a big city — San Francisco, maybe — in a fine suit with a pretty girl on your arm?"

"The city? No, I don't think that'd suit me at all. I wouldn't mind the pretty girl, though."

Rae smiled.

"You'd better mind her, if you know what's good for you."

———

They arrived at Tommy Drum's shortly after sunset and tied their horses to a hitching post near the door.

"Thank you for the escort, Mr. Garvey. Must you head back to camp immediately?"

"Not directly. I might have a taste of whiskey first."

"Tell me," she asked as they strolled towards the saloon door, tugging off their riding gloves. "Have you a first name?"

"People just call me Garvey."

"That won't do at all. What did your mother call you?"

"Well, my given name is Jim."

"James."

"Jim."

"Would you be interested in buying a pretty girl a drink, James?"

––––––––––

It was after midnight when Rae and Garvey fell into her dimly lit hotel room, drunk, laughing and tugging at each other's clothes. As they kissed, Rae pulled off Garvey's gun belt and set it next to the bed, then began working feverishly on the buttons of his pants.

"What do you think you're doing?" asked Garvey, putting up very little resistance.

"Why, I'm bone hunting, James," said Rae. "What else?"

"Oh, I see. Any luck?"

"Oh yes. I definitely found one. And it's an entirely new species."

"Really? What's it like?"

"Well, it's large. Warm blooded. And it definitely walks erect."

"Congratulations," said Garvey, pulling her back onto the bed. "You get to give it a name."

🌱

"While Miss Callahan and I were getting better acquainted," Garvey explained, "four hundred miles west of us, in Colorado, the Fates were working overtime, conspiring once again to complicate our lives."

I looked up from my notepad.

"Colorado?"

"Bear Creek, to be specific. There was a schoolteacher there named Arthur Lakes. He was English born and educated. How a dandy like that ever wound up in Colorado is beyond me. I asked him once, but never got a clear answer. The man talked in such a roundabout way, by the time he got around to it I'd lost all interest."

"A new addition to our cast of characters?" I asked.

"And we've got a ways to go, yet."

"Please, continue."

"So, one afternoon this English schoolteacher decides to go hiking in the badlands of Colorado, and he takes a friend by the name of Captain Henry Beckwith along with him. . . ."

Chapter Fourteen

BEAR CREEK, COLORADO

"Henry? Let's take a break, shall we?"

Captain Henry Beckwith, a crusty, retired military man wearing a blue, sun-faded cavalry hat, slowed his pace to allow Arthur Lakes to catch up with him. The young schoolteacher, a British expatriate, was twenty years younger than Beckwith, but simply couldn't keep up in the heat of the afternoon sun.

Beckwith screwed the cap from his canteen and took a sip as he leaned back against the cool canyon wall.

"Excellent," said Arthur, as he took the last few exhausting steps and dragged himself to a nearby tree stump and slumped there, gasping for breath. "That last bit . . . was . . . what's the expression? A 'real arse burner'?"

"That it was," said Beckwith, chuckling. "Sure is pretty country, though."

Arthur took a long draw from his own canteen and

glanced around. "Isn't it? I find it fascinating."

"Fascinating? That's an odd choice of words, Artie. I didn't say it was fascinating. I said it was pretty."

"Well, yes, of course. But it's also fascinating."

"All right. I'll bite. How do you figure it's fascinating?"

"Well, for starters . . . that canyon wall." Arthur motioned to the layered tiers of yellow, brown, and gray in the sandstone wall behind Beckwith. "Just look at it. A remarkably fine representation of the stratified rocks of the Triassic, Jurassic, and Cretaceous periods."

"It's a rock with some wavy lines in it."

"Precisely! The wavy, irregular character of the bedding is undoubtedly the result of angry waves. This was once the shore of a vast inland sea."

Beckwith sighed. "Artie, if you don't stop gabbin' on, I'll show you some angry waves."

Arthur wasn't the least bit offended. He and Beckwith were old friends and he was used to the captain's abuse. It was his way of teasing, and Arthur found it endearing.

Beckwith reached into the inside pocket of his jacket, produced a silver flask, and raised it.

"Here's to fascinating rocks!"

He took a long pull and then passed the flask. Arthur took a small sip, closed his eyes, and smiled as the warmth of the whiskey spread through him.

"I swear, this tastes entirely different when . . ."

He opened his eyes and stopped in mid-sentence. "Hello. What's this?"

Beckwith turned and followed his gaze.

Arthur approached the rock wall and brushed away

some dust, revealing a fossilized leaf embedded in the sandstone.

Beckwith shrugged. "I give up. What is it?"

"A fossilized leaf. Quite well preserved."

Unimpressed, Beckwith took another slug from the flask. "Big deal. There's a whole petrified tree stump yonder."

"Is there?" Arthur looked around. "Where?"

"Damn, Artie. You were sittin' right on it!"

Arthur looked at the tree stump he had been sitting on and examined it.

"This is too smooth to be a tree. Odd. And look at this patch. It's got a purplish hue." He brushed away some moss and other debris. "Henry, this is a bone."

"Bullshit. It's too big to be a bone."

Arthur brushed off some more debris. The top of the object was rounded off in a very distinct manner that he recognized immediately. It was most definitely a bone.

"Henry? This is the fossilized bone of some gigantic animal."

"Jesus H. Palomino. This thing must've been huge!"

"There may be more. Help me look."

Beckwith paced the area near the first bone, occasionally dropping to one knee, while Arthur approached a section of scrub covering part of the canyon wall. He pushed the brush aside, peering behind it, and froze.

"Captain Beckwith? Henry!"

Beckwith leapt to his feet and ran over.

"Lord almighty!"

There, imbedded in the sandstone wall, was the clear

outline of a fossilized vertebra.

————————

Two days later, Lakes, Beckwith, and a local blacksmith named Pease were stacking a large number of huge fossilized bones in a battered wooden cart.

Beckwith pulled up short, gripping his lower back in pain.

"Damn, Artie. I'm too creaky for all this liftin'. I don't think I can take much more."

Arthur was filled with energy. "I don't think you appreciate the value of this discovery, Captain. These are dinosaur bones. Perhaps the largest ever found!"

"I'll tell you what, my back sure appreciates it."

"I've telegraphed a famous dinosaur expert at Yale University. I'm sure we'll have help very soon."

"Well, till then you're going to have to do your digging without me. I'm sorry, Artie."

Arthur patted his friend on the shoulder sympathetically.

"Can't be helped, I suppose." He turned to the blacksmith. "What about you, Mr. Pease? Can I persuade you to stay on awhile? I could pay you a bit. Not much on a teacher's salary, I'm afraid."

"Smithing's been slow and Phyllis says I'm getting fat. Reckon I could use the exercise."

"Excellent. Good show."

Beckwith sat on a low rocky outcropping, tugged off his hat, and wiped the sweat from his brow. "Yale University, you say? What's the name of this dinosaur expert?"

"Professor Marsh."

Chapter Fifteen

THE SALINE RIVER, KANSAS

Marsh and P. T. Barnum sat at a long table covered with small, tagged fossil bones, sipping tea as Mudge approached holding a folded slip of paper.

"A telegraph," Mudge explained. "It was forwarded from New Haven."

"Let's have it, then." Marsh accepted the telegraph and unfolded it, squinting at the text.

"Bear Creek? Where in the devil is Bear Creek?"

"Morrison, Colorado," Mudge replied. "Near Boulder."

Barnum raised his cup. "Beautiful country."

"More dinosaur bones?" Marsh looked up at Mudge. "Benjamin, dinosaurs are a fascinating oddity, but evolutionary theory won't be proved or disproved by digging up reptiles. The Eocene horse, the birds of the Cretaceous—that's where our research should be directed." He turned to Barnum. "P. T., this sounds more like your sort of thing."

"No, no," the showman replied. "Dinosaurs are old hat. People have had enough of sea serpents and flying dragons. Find me something different. The next Cardiff Giant."

Marsh scoffed. "That old hoax? Nothing but humbug."

"I could use a new humbug. Find me something different, O. C., and I'll pay you handsomely for it."

"Whatever I find, you can see it with the rest of the country, on display at the Peabody Museum at Yale."

"I'd forgotten. Why would you need my money when you've got your Uncle George?"

Marsh handed the telegram back to Mudge. "File this. If things should dry up here, perhaps we'll find time to call on Mr. Lakes."

"Very good, Professor."

As Mudge headed off, Barnum finished the last of his tea. He stood and put on his hat, tipping it to Marsh.

"I have a train to catch. I've enjoyed our time together, O. C. It's been a pleasure. Good hunting!"

"And to you, P. T. May you find your humbug."

"Oh, I will. I always do."

Chapter Sixteen

MORRISON, COLORADO

Morrison, Colorado, a small, quaint town nestled in the foothills of the Rocky Mountains, consisted of a general store, a livery, a white steepled church, a modest saloon, and a number of middle class residences. The town's centerpiece was a small but pristine building that housed Jarvis Hall, a liberal arts institution.

As Arthur Lakes pulled the rickety wagonload of bones to a stop in front of the main entrance, a crowd of curious townsfolk approached. A chubby, red-faced man in a barber's apron tugged on Arthur's sleeve.

"Can we see the giant bones?"

An excited murmur passed through the crowd as they pushed closer, eager to see.

Arthur looked around nervously. "Just a moment, please!"

Before he could climb down off of the wagon, the

barber reached under the tarp and lifted the beautifully polished shaft of a bone and waved it around for all to see.

"Wow! Look at this one!"

"Please," Arthur pleaded, "be careful!"

"Whoops." The bone slipped from his grasp and fell to the hard-packed dirt of the street, breaking into several pieces.

"Stop this immediately!"

Pease leaped from the seat beside him. "Here, Mr. Lakes." He tugged a pistol from his belt and fired a shot into the air, silencing the crowd.

"Ladies and gentleman, please!" Arthur shouted. "Let us unload the bones, and I promise you'll all have a good long look at them."

Reluctantly, the crowd began to disperse.

Two grinning men emerged from the building: Joshua Smith, the president of the college, closely followed by an enthusiastic newspaperman.

"Here he is, now!" said Smith. "Arthur, this gentleman is from the *Colorado Springs Gazette*. May I introduce Professor Arthur Lakes, head of the Jarvis Hall Paleontology Department?"

Arthur looked up, confused. "Paleontology Department? I'm a bloody English teacher!"

Smith chuckled. "He's quite humble. Arthur, the gentleman would like to interview you for his paper. It would be quite good publicity for the college."

"It might even get picked up by the Associated Press," the reporter added.

"Did you hear that, Arthur? The Associated Press!"

"Yes, yes. Very nice," said Arthur. "Has there been

a telegraph for me?"

"Telegraph? No. Not that I'm aware of."

"It's been two weeks!" said Pease.

Arthur frowned. "I may have to ship Professor Marsh some samples."

"It might get his attention if he was to read about it in the papers."

Arthur looked at the reporter for a moment, then broke into a wide smile. Some publicity might work to his advantage.

"So, you're a press man, are you?" Arthur put his arm around the young man's shoulder and led him into the building, smiling congenially.

Chapter Seventeen

THE SALINE RIVER, KANSAS

The sun was beginning to set as Rae rode up to the edge of the excavation pit at the Marsh encampment. Down below, Marsh was on his knees, examining a fresh find. He looked up, saw her, and waved cheerfully. He stood, brushed the dust from his trousers, and headed up the ramp to meet her.

"Miss Callahan. How nice to see you! Can I offer you tea? One of the students can fetch it."

"No thank you, Professor."

Marsh lowered his voice, conspiratorially. "So, what news from the enemy camp?"

"Cope found some sort of flying dinosaur."

"A pterodactyl? That's nothing new."

"It's rather a large one."

"Well, I'm sure we'll survive it." He noticed her expression and frowned. "Is something wrong?"

"I . . . I'm not sure I like the spy business."

"Well, you're perfectly free to end our arrangement if you wish. Which reminds me . . ."

He handed her a small coin pouch. It was heavier than she expected. She peered inside.

"This is a lot of money."

"You're performing a valuable service."

"Well, I'm glad to help." She paused for a moment, considering, then added, "The dinosaur . . . the pterodactyl. He said it had a twenty foot wing span."

Mudge emerged from the pit and overheard this.

"Good Lord," he exclaimed. "Twenty foot?"

Marsh scowled. "This is catastrophic."

"What about you, Professor?" Rae asked. "Have you found anything?"

Mudge answered for him. "Only the find of his career!"

Marsh shot him a look. "It's probably nothing of the kind."

Rae looked to Mudge for his reaction. He looked away quickly, his face reddening. "Yes, I'm sure it's nothing."

Rae raised her eyebrows, unconvinced. "Well, that is a shame."

Marsh quickly changed the subject. "We're losing the light, Benjamin. Let's break for the evening. Whatever it is, it can wait until daybreak."

"Do you mind if I return in the morning?" Rae asked. "I'm anxious to see what you've found."

Marsh stammered, "Well, I don't know . . . I mean I'm sure it's . . ."

Rae took his arm and leaned in, gently stroking his beard with her finger.

"O. C., do you not trust me?"

Marsh was weakening. "I suppose . . . it would be all right . . ."

Rae smiled sweetly.

"Until tomorrow, then." She pecked him on the cheek, mounted her horse, and rode off.

A short time later, Rae met with Garvey, Sternberg, and Cope inside the tent that served as their own encampment's command center.

"The find of his career?" Cope was saying. "What could it be?"

"He's not sure," said Rae. "They lost the light and had to stop for the night."

"I'll tell you, if it were me, I'd be digging by torchlight."

Garvey rubbed his chin. "Why not do just that?"

Cope looked at him. "What?"

"Well, it ain't like Marsh owns the plains. If he ain't there, there's no reason we can't go have a look ourselves."

Cope smiled slyly.

"They're snoring like buzz saws," said Garvey. "Don't look like they got any kind of guards at all. Must feel pretty confident."

It was well past midnight. Cope, Sternberg, Garvey, and Rae were hiding in the shadows at the perimeter of the Marsh encampment.

"Quickly," said Cope. "Let's get to work!"

They crept silently down the ramp into Marsh's excavation pit carrying shielded lanterns and digging equipment.

"It's over near those rocks," Rae whispered.

"Hurry," said Cope. We must be out of here before dawn."

Less than an hour later, Garvey and Sternberg carefully inched up the ramp carrying a heavy object wrapped in cloth. Cope and Rae followed. They were all filthy and exhausted.

———————

Back in Cope's tent, the unwrapped fossil sat in the center of the table, illuminated by candlelight.

"I've never seen anything like it," Cope marveled.

It was the skull of a small dinosaur, but in addition to rows of razor-sharp teeth, it had two large canine fangs.

"It looks like a *Hadrosaurus* skull," Sternberg offered.

Cope shook his head. "But *Hadrosaurus* was a duck-billed plant eater. Look at those teeth! They look almost canine! This is a carnivore."

Sternberg shook his head in amazement. "Incredible."

Cope turned to Garvey and Rae. "You should get some sleep. Tomorrow will be a busy day."

"What about you?" Garvey asked.

"I'll never be able to sleep," said Cope. "I must write this up immediately. If there are more of these around, Marsh may find one and publish first."

———————

By the time Garvey awoke in his tent, the sun had already risen. He looked down and saw Rae, sound asleep, wrapped in the crook of his arm. He watched her for a few moments until she stirred. She stretched and opened her eyes blearily. She saw that he was looking at her, and narrowed her eyes.

"What?"

"Just looking at you, is all," said Garvey, smiling. "Don't go and spoil the moment."

She returned his smile, and then yawned. "What time is it?"

"Late."

"I have to go."

Rae sat up and began pulling on her clothes.

"Where's the fire, darlin'?"

"Marsh invited me to come to his camp this morning. If I don't show, he'll be suspicious."

———

As Rae approached the Marsh encampment, she heard laughter coming from the excavation pit.

"Wait, wait!" It was Marsh's voice. "We must have a toast!"

She rushed down the ramp and found Marsh, Mudge, and the Yale students gathered in celebration. Mudge was dutifully filling glasses with champagne, and all of them were grinning.

Marsh raised his glass.

"To Professor Cope's latest discovery, *Hadrosaurus humbugus*!"

They all raised their glasses and shouted in unison.

"*Hadrosaurus humbugus!*"

Laughter, cheers, and a chorus of "hear-hears" rang out, and they drank.

"I don't believe my ears!" They turned to see Rae approaching, her face twisted in a scowl.

"Miss Callahan!" said Marsh, grinning broadly. "Champagne?"

"That skull was a fake?"

"Oh, the skull was quite real. As were the teeth. They just happened to be from two completely different specimens." Marsh refilled his champagne glass. "It will take Cope weeks to discover our little ruse, if he does at all!"

"Do you really think he'll publish it?" Mudge asked.

"Oh, I do hope so!" Marsh replied. "That, coupled with his wrong-ended *Mosasaurus*, would make him a laughingstock for years to come!"

"You used me," Rae spat.

"Certainly, I used you. You were in my employ. You were also in the employ of Professor Cope, from what I gather. You seem to know quite a lot about using people."

"You go straight to hell!"

"If I hear there are interesting fossils there, I'll make it my next stop." Marsh softened his voice. "Miss Callahan. Rae. Now that everything's out in the open, you have a choice to make. You can rush back to Cope and tell him about the trick I've played. He'll be grateful for awhile, I'm sure. But then, what? You'll be of no more use as a spy. That's not a problem for me. I have another . . . employee in Cope's camp. But Cope will never trust you again. You'll be worthless to him."

"And what might you suggest I do?"

"Don't tell him. Keep taking his money and continue working for me."

"I'm through being your spy."

"There is a third option," said Marsh. "You're a very beautiful, very bright young woman, Miss Callahan. Come back to Connecticut with me. I'm a very wealthy man. I'll treat you like a princess." Marsh swallowed, then quite sincerely said, "I could make you very happy, Miss Callahan."

"I'm sorry, O.C.," she replied with equal sincerity. "That will never happen. I don't have feelings for you."

"You could learn."

She shook her head. "You're wrong. I'm sorry."

She turned and left without another word.

Mudge put his hand on Marsh's shoulder. "She'll tell Cope."

"Undoubtedly." He shook his head, sadly. "But she'll be back, mark my words. Garvey is an uneducated thug. That cowboy won't be able to hang on to a fiery beauty like that."

———

Rae rode directly back to the Cope encampment and headed for the main tent.

Inside, Sternberg and Cope were seated at the table examining the altered skull alongside a normal hadrosaur skull. Garvey sat on the far side of the tent, pitching cards one by one into his upturned hat.

Cope shook his head. "This makes absolutely no sense."

Sternberg nodded in agreement. "Indeed."

"How could two animals with virtually identical craniums develop along such divergent paths?"

Rae spoke up. "They couldn't."

Cope turned. "Excuse me?"

Garvey stopped pitching cards and looked up. Rae took a deep breath and continued. "The teeth in that skull are from a different animal."

"How could you possibly . . ." Cope stopped in mid-sentence as the realization struck him. "Marsh!"

"He knows I'm working for you. He set it up to make you look foolish." Rae took another deep breath. "That's not all."

"What is it, Rae?"

"I wanted you to hear this from me. When I came to your camp, I was already working for Marsh. I . . . I told him about the flying dinosaur."

Cope's face grew red. "What? Does he have one?"

"I don't believe so."

"Thank God ours has already been shipped! There's no harm done, then."

Rae looked ashamed. "Isn't there?"

"Miss Callahan. We are far from perfect creatures. Every one of us has done things we regret. You've come clean now, and that's good enough for me."

Sternberg bent over and carefully examined the skull with the implanted teeth. "You know, it's not a bad skull actually. They did do some damage forcing the teeth . . ."

"What sort of second-rate scientist damages a priceless

fossil, just to effect some sort of juvenile prank?"

Sternberg chuckled. "Wish you'd thought of it?"

Cope answered instantly. "It would have been exquisite."

Garvey glared at Rae. Her eyes shifted nervously, avoiding his angry gaze.

"Professor," Rae continued, "Marsh said I wasn't his only spy. He said he had another employee in this camp."

Cope frowned. "A traitor among us? That is worrisome."

"I think you mean *another* traitor." Garvey stood and grabbed his hat. "I need some air. It stinks in here."

He headed out of the tent. Rae rushed after him. "James . . ."

Garvey ignored her and mounted his horse.

"James! Wait, please!"

He whipped the horse around and glared down at her. "It's one thing you were spying for Marsh. I done some things in my life I ain't proud of, too. But you lied to me, Rae. You lied to all of us. Now, how am I gonna know what's true and what ain't?"

"Where are you going?"

"To town. I got some thinkin' to do, and I ain't up for it, so I'm gonna get drunk instead."

He turned and rode off without looking back.

Chapter Eighteen

HAYS CITY, KANSAS

Garvey tied his horse to the hitching post outside Tommy Drum's Saloon and walked to a nearby water trough. He bent over and dunked his head, then shook the water from his hair and set his hat back on his head. He took a deep breath and stared at his reflection on the still-rippling surface of the trough.

As the water settled, he noticed something in the reflection. Behind him, Lucas, one of the new diggers at the Cope camp, was walking towards the saloon. Lucas stopped near the door for a moment, looked around guiltily, and then headed around the side of a building.

Garvey followed, being careful to remain out of sight. Peering around the corner, he saw Lucas a short distance away talking conspiratorially with another figure partially obstructed from view by the wall of the building. Lucas handed him something. The man nodded, and Lucas headed off.

Garvey turned his back as Lucas passed by, and waited. A moment later, a second man left the alley. As he passed, Garvey looked at the water trough and saw the man's reflected face.

It was Marsh.

———————

Several hours later, Garvey sat at a table in the mostly empty saloon with a half-empty bottle of whiskey before him.

Another voice drifted across the room. "Gimme a whiskey."

Garvey turned to look. It was Lucas, standing at the bar. He caught sight of Garvey and smiled. "Hey, Garv. How's tricks?"

Garvey smiled broadly and stood. He swaggered towards Lucas, more than a little drunk.

"Tricks?" Garvey asked.

Lucas chuckled, uneasily. "Had a couple, huh?"

"Here's a trick."

Garvey grabbed the shocked man by the collar and threw him across the room, knocking over several tables. Lucas groaned and sat up, dazed, blood trickling from his lip.

"You're Marsh's spy, aren't you? You goddamned snake."

Lucas wiped his chin and looked at the blood on his hand. Suddenly, Lucas was on his feet, charging in low. He slammed Garvey back against the bar.

Garvey boxed his ears and punched Lucas in the gut. Lucas staggered back, then grabbed a chair and threw it. Garvey sidestepped. The chair sailed over the bar and shattered a row of bottles.

Tommy Drum backed away and shouted to another saloon worker. "Get the sheriff!"

Garvey rushed Lucas again, knocking over more tables.

———————

As early morning light filtered across his face, Garvey moaned and opened his eyes. He was in a jail cell, and he was battered and bloody. The cell door was open, and a deputy sat with his feet on a desk, reading a newspaper. He spoke without looking up.

"Mornin' sunshine."

Garvey spat blood and checked his mouth for broken teeth.

"What's good about it?"

He looked around the cell. He was its only occupant.

"Where's Lucas?"

"Long gone. You're free to go too, if you're sobered up."

Garvey stood, wincing at the pain in his head. The deputy smiled and returned to his newspaper. "Figured you needed to sleep off that whiskey."

Garvey splashed water from a wash basin into his face and leaned against the wall, steadying himself. He glanced over, noticing the headline on the deputy's newspaper, partially obscured where it was folded in half. It read "THE BONES OF MONSTERS . . ."

He blinked and tried to focus on it.

"You done readin' that first page there?"

The deputy peeled off the first page off the paper and set it on the desk.

"Help yourself."

Garvey lifted it and looked at the story. The full headline read:

THE BONES OF MONSTERS
COLORADO SCHOOLTEACHER FINDS MONSTROUS ANIMAL BONES NEAR MORRISON!

"Did Lucas see this paper?"

"Matter of fact, yeah. He asked where he could buy a copy."

"Son of a bitch." Garvey grabbed his hat from a wall peg and put it on. "Thanks for your hospitality," he said, without much sincerity.

"It's what I do," said the deputy, without looking up from his paper.

———

"A femur fourteen inches across at its *base*?"

Sternberg was reading the article over Cope's shoulder in the main tent while Garvey sat drinking strong coffee.

"That's what it says," Garvey replied. "Is that unusual?"

"Mr. Garvey, with a femur that size, this animal would have to be sixty to seventy feet long!"

Garvey whistled in amazement.

"Does Marsh know about this?" asked Cope.

"Looks like it," said Garvey.

Sternberg shook his head. "It's like nothing we've ever seen!"

"Damn," muttered Cope. He thought for a moment, coming to a decision. "Charles, telegraph Mr. Lakes immediately. Wire him money if you have to. I want those bones." He turned to Garvey. "How long will it take to pack up the camp?"

"Three, four hours, maybe."

"Make it two. We need to catch the next train." He looked at the paper again, and then looked up, grinning broadly. "Gentlemen, we are bound for Colorado!"

—————

"What do you mean, there are no tickets?"

"Just what I said."

Cope looked around him. The train platform was virtually empty. He slammed his fist on the counter in frustration. "But . . . but . . . how can that be?"

"Some gent with a beard pulled out a big bankroll and bought out the whole train—lock, stock, and barrel."

"What?!"

Now a familiar voice said, "Why, hello, Edward!"

Cope turned, his face flush with anger. Marsh was strolling by, tugging on a pair of leather gloves. Behind him, Mudge, Lucas, and the Yalies were carrying crates of equipment to the freight car.

"Lovely day for traveling, don't you think?"

"You unprincipled, egotistical . . ."

Marsh smiled. "I'd love to stay and chat, but I have a train to catch. Ta!"

Cope turned back to the ticket seller. "When's the next westbound train?"

"Six hours."

"I assume there are tickets available?"

"All you want."

Cope pulled out his billfold and began to angrily count out the money.

Sternberg had set up several empty bottles on a tree stump a short distance from the railroad tracks. Cope raised a shaky pistol for target practice.

"One moment, Professor, one moment!" said Sternberg, rushing to get out of the line of fire to stand behind Cope. "Now remember . . ." he began.

But Cope fired before he could finish. The shot was wide.

"That was close, I think. Try again."

He fired a second shot. Still nothing.

Over on the train platform, Rae and Garvey relaxed on a pile of luggage. Garvey lay against a large satchel with his hat over his eyes. He lifted the brim a bit when he heard more shots from Cope, but none of them were followed by the sound of breaking glass. Garvey shook his head and returned the hat to its former position.

"I'm sorry I lied to you," Rae suddenly blurted.

Garvey lifted his hat again and looked at her, surprised.

"Well," he said awkwardly, "that's okay, I guess. You're a woman. I s'pose it's your nature."

She instantly snapped at him. "And what would you be meaning by that?!"

Garvey shrugged. "I don't know. Just seems like women need to lie more to get on in life. I ain't sayin' it's their fault or nothin'."

"That is quite probably the most ignorant thing I've ever heard you say."

Now Cope and Sternberg approached, taking a break from target practice. In the distance, the unscathed bottles appeared visibly relieved.

Cope looked at the pistol in his hand and shook his head. "There's something wrong with this gun, I think."

Sternberg took it from him and began to reload it. Garvey and Rae continued their heated discussion.

"See, that's the other thing women are good at."

"And what would that be?"

"Here I was, mad at you. And in the blink of an eye you got it all turned around so I'm feeling bad 'cause you're mad at me. They teach you to do that in woman school or something?"

"You're feeling bad?"

"Well, yeah."

"Good." She stood and strolled smugly down the platform. Cope and Sternberg desperately tried not to chuckle.

"I swear . . ."

"I've heard it said that there are two ways to argue with a woman, Mr. Garvey," said Cope. "I've also heard that neither of them works."

"You couldn't stop that one with a forty-foot rope and a snubbin' post, that's for certain."

"She's coming, isn't she?"

Garvey shrugged. "I expect she is." He pulled his hat back over his eyes. "I may have a short rope, but I throw a wide loop."

Cope chuckled. From the platform, Sternberg turned towards the bottles and raised the reloaded pistol. One of the bottles shattered.

Cope shook his head. "Hmph."

Sternberg looked slightly embarrassed. Garvey smiled without raising the hat from his eyes.

Chapter Nineteen

MORRISON, COLORADO

Classes had ended for the day, and Arthur Lakes pushed through the small crowd of Jarvis Hall students with an armload of paperwork to find Cope and Sternberg waiting for him outside.

"Mr. Lakes?" asked Cope.

"Yes?"

"I'm Professor Cope. I telegraphed?"

Arthur smiled broadly and pumped Cope's hand. "Professor Cope! Yes, I've read your work. How wonderful to meet you."

"Did you get the money I wired?"

"Yes, I did. Most generous, but I'm afraid I can't accept it."

"Why not?"

"I'm afraid I've already struck up an agreement with Professor Marsh. His telegraph arrived several hours prior to yours."

"I'll double whatever he's paying."

"That's quite generous, but of course, it is about science, isn't it? Professor Marsh and I have a gentleman's agreement. I am a man of my word."

"Of course you are, of course you are. Can we at least have a look at the fossils?"

"Professor Marsh had them shipped to Yale almost immediately, I'm afraid. I really must run. I'm due at the site."

"Yes, well. Good digging."

"Delighted to meet you. Smashing. Really."

Arthur hurried off with a wave.

"What now?" said Sternberg.

"There was another man mentioned in the newspaper, wasn't there? A retired military man? Captain Beckwith?"

———

Captain Beckwith was feeding the chickens that roamed his front yard as Cope and Sternberg rode up.

"Captain Beckwith. Do you have a moment, sir?"

"Well, now. That's something you can never be sure of. I try to live my life like I might not."

"You're a wise man," said Cope. And a war hero, I understand. This country owes you a great debt."

"Well, tell 'em I'd like it in small bills."

Cope laughed politely and introduced himself. "I'm Professor Cope. This is my associate, Mr. Sternberg."

"Professor, huh? You must be that feller from Yale that Arthur was telling me about."

"Um . . . yes. Yes, that's exactly right . . ."

Sternberg looked confused and opened his mouth to say something. Cope shot him a stern look and raised his voice to make his intentions clear.

"We're from *Yale University*."

Now Sternberg nodded in understanding and played along.

"Yes! Quite correct! We're . . . helping to excavate the fossil bones."

"Well, I'm glad you're here. Arthur sure could use the help. I'm having back trouble these days. It's all I can do to keep these yardbirds fed. Say, will you be seeing Arthur anytime soon?"

"Why, yes. In fact, we saw him in town not half an hour ago."

"Well, let him know that I was riding out by Oil Creek and seen some more."

"More . . . ?"

"Bones. A whole big bunch. Looks like easier diggin', too."

"Oil Creek you say?"

Sternberg pulled out a pencil and paper. "Where is that, exactly?"

Chapter Twenty

BEAR CREEK QUARRY, COLORADO

"Just incredible! Can you imagine the size of these creatures?"

Marsh and Arthur Lakes were standing before a table with a huge bone atop it. It was the largest fossil yet. Behind him, Mudge and the Yale students were hard at work, excavating more.

Lakes nodded in agreement. "I'm so pleased to have someone here who appreciates them, Professor."

Now Mudge approached them, wiping sweat from his brow with a handkerchief.

"Lord, this is hard ground. We've been excavating all day, with just this single bone to show for it."

"But what a bone!" said Marsh.

A horse and rider approached and Mr. Pease, the blacksmith, dismounted and tipped his hat. His face was grim.

"Bad news, Mr. Lakes."

"Bad news?" said Lakes.

"There're more diggers in the area."

"Oh yes," said Lakes, waving a dismissing hand. "I met them in town. Mr. Cope and Mr. Sternberg."

Marsh looked horrified. "Cope? He's here?"

"He came by the college a few days ago. Nice chap. Do you know him?"

"You could say that."

"They're digging down by Oil Creek," said Pease.

"Have they found anything?" Marsh asked.

"Looks like they've found a bunch. And it's softer ground down there."

"Damn him!"

"There are plenty of fossils here, Professor," said Mudge. "It's just slow going with rock this hard."

Marsh considered this for a moment.

"Then we'll have to hire more workers and double our efforts!"

————

The next few weeks were a whirlwind of activity as both camps drew more and more fossils out of the earth. Newspapers across the country were picking up the stories and running them with sensational headlines:

MORE MONSTER BONES DISCOVERED!

DISTINGUISHED PROFESSORS COMPETE FOR DINOSAUR BONES!

WHO WILL FIND THE NEXT SAURIAN SKELETON?

With all the excitement in the media, dinosaur fever was sweeping the nation, and Marsh's showman friend P. T. Barnum could only stay away for so long.

On the afternoon of Barnum's arrival at the Marsh encampment, Arthur Lakes had set up an artist's easel in the shade of a tree and was painting a fairly accurate watercolor of Marsh seated on a rock contemplating several of the larger specimens. He looked up when he heard the familiar voice.

"O. C.?" Barnum shouted. "Where is that scoundrel?"

Marsh stood and broke into a wide grin. "P. T.! You old humbug!"

Barnum whistled at the specimens as he approached. "You've been busy, I see."

"Nothing you haven't read about in the papers, surely."

"Well, that's why I'm here."

Marsh motioned to a table set up in the shade beneath a canvas tarp. "Come. Let's have a drink."

———

Marsh and Barnum sat at the main specimen table sipping brandy and smoking cigars.

"Let me get this straight," said Marsh. "You want me to sell you a skeleton?"

"It's these new finds, O. C. They've captured the public imagination. Dinosaurs are popular again!"

"You must be joking."

"I've never been more serious. I'll pay you handsomely. I'll even give you a cut of the box office."

Marsh shook his head. "You know me better than that."

Barnum narrowed his eyes and puffed his cigar. "Now, don't make me go to your competitor."

"Cope?" Marsh scoffed. "Ha! He may be a poor scientist, but he won't sell fossils for a sideshow, I promise you."

Barnum rolled the cigar between his thumb and forefinger, absently gazing at its glowing tip.

"Every man's occupation should be beneficial to his fellow man, O. C. I'll give you that. But it should also be profitable to himself. All else . . . well, it's vanity and folly."

"On that point we disagree. I'm no mercenary. And whatever I think of him, neither is Cope. I'll stake my reputation on it."

Barnum smiled, downed the last of his drink, and stood.

"I'll have my dinosaur skeleton, O. C. I can promise you that. Thank you for your time and your hospitality. We'll talk soon."

With a tip of his hat he walked off, leaving Marsh with a worried look on his face.

Chapter Twenty-One

OIL CREEK, COLORADO

Rae sipped water from a ladle and then splashed her face, washing away the dust and sweat. She dropped the ladle back into the water bucket and looked up, squinting into the sun.

A short distance away, Garvey and Cope were shaking hands with P. T. Barnum. Barnum clapped Cope on the back and the two headed for the main tent. Garvey tipped his hat and left them to their discussion. He approached Rae.

"What in the devil is P. T. Barnum doing here?" she asked.

"Don't that beat all?" said Garvey. "He sure gets around."

"What did he want?"

Garvey grabbed the ladle from the bucket and took a big gulp.

"He got it in his head that he'd like a dinosaur skeleton for his sideshow. He's out here trying to talk the two professors into selling him one."

"Is he offering much money?"

"A whole passel, I expect. Ol' Barnum got more money than God these days."

"What did Professor Cope say?"

"What do you think? The professor's a scientist, not a circus man."

Rae considered for a moment.

"What if we were to sell him one?"

"What?"

"It wouldn't have to be a rare one. We could give him one of the more common types."

"You mean steal one?"

"Of course not! In case you haven't noticed, the ground out here is full of them. What's to stop us from doing a little torchlight digging for ourselves? Cope doesn't own these bones any more than he owns that creek, or those trees."

"No, he doesn't. But he does own our trust and friendship."

"James, he pays you forty dollars a week. Some big museum back east is going to make him rich for finding these bones. Do you think he'll consider your friendship when that money starts to roll in?"

"I'm done discussin' this, Rae. You want to go dig yourself up a dinosaur and sell it to the circus, you go on ahead. You'll do it without me."

Rae lowered her voice and touched his arm. "I'm just talking, James. That's all. Relax. We're partners.

If you don't want to, then we won't."

"I swear, Rae . . ."

She leaned in and gave him a quick kiss.

Garvey smiled. "Partners, huh?

"Partners."

"C'mere." He grabbed her around the waist, kissing her warmly and deeply.

Chapter Twenty-Two

BEAR CREEK QUARRY, COLORADO

Four of the Yale students looked on nervously as Pease and Lucas adjusted several banded strips of dynamite attached to a long spool of fuse.

Arthur Lakes approached. His eyes widened at the sight of the dynamite.

"Good heavens. Is that an explosive?"

"Yup," said Pease. "No small firecracker, neither."

Pease carefully lowered the dynamite into a crack in the bluff.

"Does the professor know about this?"

Lucas looked up. "It was his idea."

"He said we ain't movin' fast enough," said Pease, "and Cope's gettin' all the monster bones."

———

Lakes found Marsh and Mudge in the center of

the camp, studying a topographical map. Mudge was tapping a spot and pointing to the hillside.

"Right about there."

Marsh nodded in agreement and rolled up the map.

"Professor Marsh?" asked Lakes. "Am I to understand that you've decided to use explosives on the hillside?"

Marsh nodded. "There's a particular section that will take weeks to clear. I strongly suspect that our best samples will be found beyond it."

"Professor," said Lakes, "that sandstone is completely unpredictable."

"We're only trying it on a small section," Marsh replied. "If it seems to weaken the bluff, we'll refrain from using any more."

"Well, shouldn't the students be evacuated at the very least?"

They were all distracted by a soft explosion. A huge mushroom cloud of brown dust rose from the base of the bluff. The cheers of the Yalies echoed across the quarry.

Marsh smiled. "There, you see?"

A moment later, a low rumbling began. It grew louder, building in intensity.

"What's happening?" Mudge shouted.

As the three rushed towards the still-rising cloud of dust, the entire top of the bluff began to collapse.

"My God!" Marsh shouted. "Get out of there!"

The Yale students scattered, running from the avalanche in all directions. Several of them were knocked off their feet, and in seconds they were buried by the enormous expanding cloud of debris.

At that moment, the rumbling reached the Oil Creek site. Cope looked up to see the distant cloud of dust.

"Marsh has had a collapse!" He turned to Sternberg. "Quickly! Gather everyone. There may be injuries!"

Garvey shouted to Rae. "Rae, see if you can't scare up some bandages!"

She nodded and ran towards the tents. Garvey leapt on his horse as Sternberg rode up alongside him, followed by several of their hired diggers.

"Let's move, Charlie!"

The horses thundered out of the camp, heading towards the rising dust in the distance.

When Rae arrived, the Marsh encampment looked like a war zone. She immediately rolled up her sleeves to attend to the injured.

When she finished wiping the brow of one of the injured Yalies, she moved down the line to the next man. It was Lucas, the digger who betrayed Cope and was now working for Marsh. He was partially covered by a blood-stained blanket and his face ran with cold sweat. He was obviously in excruciating pain.

Lucas smiled weakly. "Howdy, Miss Rae. Reckon I deserved this. I don't expect I'll be diggin' up any more bones for Mr. Cope or Mr. Marsh."

Rae rung out a wet cloth and placed it on his forehead. "Hush now."

She raised one end of the blanket to look at his injuries, grimaced, and slowly lowered it.

"How bad is it?" Lucas asked.

"It's not good," she replied.

Now Garvey appeared. He smiled at Lucas. "You'll be okay, you little cow turd. You still owe me a rematch."

"I expect we'll have to have that rematch in the next world, Garv." Lucas closed his eyes for a moment as a wave of pain passed through him. "You still sore at me?"

"Naw. I'm over it. Holdin' a grudge is like drinkin' poison and expecting someone else to die."

"I'm glad of that. I thought you was still sore."

Lucas sucked in a breath as another wave of pain crested. The breath caught in his throat, and his eyes went wide. It was his last breath.

Rae looks up at Garvey with tear-filled eyes. After a moment, she wiped them and lifted the blanket over Lucas's head, then moved on to the next patient.

————

Mudge and Arthur Lakes gently set the body of one of the students on a flatbed wagon as Marsh and Cope looked on.

"This is tragic. Absolutely tragic."

"How many are dead?" asked Cope.

Lakes began to list them. "Mr. Pease, the blacksmith. At least two of the students . . ."

"Three students," said Marsh. "And Mr. Lucas."

"That makes five," said Cope, shaking his head sadly.

"Edward," said Marsh. "I must thank you for your help."

"We're gentleman, Othniel. You would have done the same."

"I would," said Marsh. He turned and looked at the collapsed wall of the quarry. "It's gone. All of it. I got impatient, Edward. I tried to take the easy route. But there are no shortcuts in science. Good men are dead because I let my ambition get the better of me."

"You mustn't blame yourself."

"Mustn't I? We can both learn from this, Edward."

"Well, you'll be happy to hear that the Oil Creek site is finally drying up."

Marsh smiled slightly. "You might be a gentleman, but you're a poor liar." He turned to Mudge. "Benjamin, let's get these injured men to a doctor. Then, let's go get good and drunk."

Mudge looked at Marsh with tired eyes. "I'm leaving, O. C."

"What?"

"I'm tired. Tired of the heat, tired of the dust, tired of adventures. I'm going back to New Haven."

"Benjamin, are you certain?"

"It's something I've been thinking about for some time. There's plenty of work back at the university. Crates and crates of fossils to unpack."

Marsh put his hand on his friend's shoulder. "You'll be greatly missed, Benjamin. But I understand. I won't stop you." He turned to Lakes. "What about you, Arthur? Are you tired of adventures?"

"I've had quite enough for one day, to be sure. But there's always tomorrow."

"Yes. Yes, I suppose there is."

Chapter Twenty-Three

MORRISON, COLORADO

A rickety cart covered with tarps rattled down Morrison's main thoroughfare, drawn by two anemic-looking mules. The cart was driven by Reed, a rodent-faced man with small, dark eyes. He wore a shabby bowler cap and a black coat several sizes too large. His partner Carlin, a coarse, insolent-looking man with the fancy two-gun rig of a gunslinger, rode a black mare alongside the wagon.

Marsh and Arthur Lakes sat at a table in the saloon getting sullenly drunk as the wagon pulled up outside. A moment later Carlin entered with Reed shadowing him. He looked around the bar and spotted Marsh and Lakes. He smiled, revealing a gold-capped front tooth, and approached.

"Is one of you named Marsh?"

"That would be me," Marsh replied as he refilled

his whiskey glass from a half-empty bottle.

"Care to step outside?" Carlin asked.

Marsh looked up. He was too drunk to be intimidated and too depressed to care. "Oh, just shoot me and be done with it."

Carlin looked confused. "I ain't aiming to shoot you, sir."

"Well, then sit. Have a drink."

Carlin's grin returned. "I wouldn't mind." He spun a chair around and straddled it, signaling Reed to join him.

"Name's Carlin. This is Reed."

Reed nodded without expression. "Howdy."

"We're railroad workers from Wyoming. We come a long way to see you."

"Really," said Marsh, blearily. "Why is that?"

"Well, I reckon we found the biggest cash-shay of dinosaur bones you ever seen."

Marsh smiled doubtfully. "Have you, now?"

"That is a fact."

"And you say you work the railroads?"

Reed giggled at this. "Oh, we work 'em all right."

Carlin shot Reed a look, shutting him up.

"If you'd care to step outside, we got us a cartful, sittin' right out front."

Marsh looked at Lakes, then shrugged. "Why not?"

———

The four men approached the cart. Carlin reached out and tugged the tarp out of the way, revealing their cargo. Marsh's eyes went wide. He looked like a man who had found his grail.

Carlin squinted at him. "So? What do you think?"

"I . . . I think . . ." Marsh stammered, "you have some fine specimens here."

The bones were enormous. Even larger than the Bear Creek specimens. Lakes touched one, then noticed something and leaned for a closer look. Many of them had fresh scratches and gash marks on them.

"These have been damaged."

"What happened to them?"

Carlin shot Reed another disapproving look. "Carelessness, I reckon."

Reed shrugged and tried to defend himself. "It's hard work diggin' them up! Sometimes the pick axe'll slip up a bit."

Marsh looked horrified. "Pick ax?!!"

"Well, hell," said Reed. "You want more? There's a whole passel of 'em!"

"Hold your tongue, Reed" snapped Carlin. "I'm negotiatin' here!"

Marsh licked his lips. "There are more of these?"

"That's what we come to talk with you about. There's a whole big area. A dry lake bed. It's full of 'em!"

"How big an area?"

"Oh, six . . . seven miles."

"Seven *miles*?" Marsh looked at Lakes, who raised his eyebrows in hopeful anticipation. "Gentleman, I believe we can come to an arrangement."

Chapter Twenty-Four

COMO BLUFF, WYOMING TERRITORY

Three days later, Marsh and Lakes stepped over the top of a bluff and gazed across the dry lake bed. They froze, mouths agape. After a moment, Marsh's stunned expression became a smile, then a chuckle, and finally a gleefully sinister laugh.

The plain, stretching for miles and miles, was dotted with huge, partially buried bones, ribs, and skulls. It was like an enormous prehistoric graveyard of bones.

"Gents," said Carlin, appearing behind them. "Welcome to Como Bluff!"

———————

Several hours later, Marsh and Lake were surrounded by several piles of recently excavated bones. Marsh was simply overwhelmed.

"It's been less than a day," he marveled, "and already

I've seen three entirely new Jurassic species! It's a gold mine! A literal gold mine!"

"Professor," said Lakes, "we simply can't do all this work by ourselves. We need more diggers."

"I expected you might."

They turned in the direction of the voice. Carlin and Reed had arrived on horseback with a motley group of gunslingers and bad men. The twenty-plus desperadoes were chewing tobacco, spitting, scratching, and generally looking menacing.

"My heavens," said Lakes.

"These're some friends of ours," Carlin offered. "They're all willin' to pitch in with your gold mine, provided you're willin' to pay."

Marsh swallowed nervously. They were all wearing guns.

"I don't think these are the sort of men that would take rejection well," Lakes whispered. "They look a bit on the rough and boorish side."

"Point well taken," Marsh agreed. He raised his voice and spoke to the group. "I can pay forty dollars a month."

The men grumbled among themselves. A few of them snickered.

"Well, sir," said Carlin. "I reckon you'd better make that a hundred and forty."

"Each?" said Lakes, astonished.

Marsh shook his head. "I simply can't afford that, gentlemen. I'll tell you what. I'll make it ninety."

"Ninety dollars?" said Reed. "That's a heap of money, Carlin."

"Shut up, Reed!" He turned back to Marsh. "We ain't stupid, Professor! We know you stand to make a killin' with these here bones."

Marsh thought for a moment, and then said, "In a month's time, if the find provides me with a substantial increase in capital, I'll increase your salary. Fair enough?"

"That sounds fair," said Reed.

A number of the men mumbled their agreement. Carlin wasn't one of them.

"I told you to shut up, Reed!"

"I was only sayin' . . ."

"I said shut up!" He wheeled on Marsh. "I guess you can just dig up them bones by yourselves, then. Hope nothin' happens to them in the meanwhile." He shouted to the desperadoes. "Come on, boys!"

About half of the men spun their horses to join Carlin. Reed and the rest didn't move.

"I said, come on!" shouted Carlin.

Reed shook his head. "We're stayin', Carlin. Ninety dollars is a fair wage. Hell, the marshal in Medicine Bow don't make but sixty!"

"You crossin' me, Reed?"

"I reckon I am."

Reed drew his pistol. Instantly, all of the men drew their own. It was a standoff between the two groups: Carlin's men against Reed's men.

Marsh held up his hands. "Gentleman! Please! There's no call for violence!"

"You're in the territories, Marsh!" Carlin spat. "There's always a call for violence." He turned to Reed's group. "You know, he ain't the only one looking for bones. The newspaper said there's another bone hunter. What's his name? Cope? I expect he'll pay what we're asking."

"I need the money now," said Reed. "I got debts with some rough customers."

"Hell, we all do!" said Carlin. "Cope'll pay. I guarantee it. Unless Marsh here wants to change his mind?"

"I will not submit to extortion!" said Marsh.

Lakes lowered his voice. "Professor, if Cope—"

"We'll deal with Cope if we must," Marsh told him. "But if we give in to his demands, there'll be no end to it." Marsh turned to Reed. "Can I count on the loyalty of you and your men, Reed?"

Reed eyed Carlin warily. "I expect so," he replied.

"Then put away your guns and let's get to work."

Reed nodded to his men and they holstered their weapons. Carlin and his men reluctantly did the same, but Carlin was seething. "This ain't the last of it!" He turned to Reed. "And you! I'll see you get yours, you yellow-bellied traitor!"

Carlin and his men spun their horses around and rode off.

Cope and his company were met at the station by Carlin and his desperadoes. As Sternberg dispersed money to each of them, Carlin perused a written document.

"It's a standard contract," Cope explained.

Carlin shrugged. "Looks okay, I guess."

"Just sign here."

Carlin used one of his men's backs as a writing desk to sign the contract. Rae and Garvey stood behind the group watching the money change hands. She frowned, and shot a disapproving look at Garvey.

"One hundred and forty dollars each?" she whispered. "That's more than three times your salary!"

He shrugged. "It's what I agreed to."

"Then you're a fool." She picked up her suitcase and headed off in a huff.

Garvey rolled his eyes and went after her. "Rae, be reasonable. . . ."

———

The coming days were a blur. More huge skeletons were uncovered at both sites. Armed desperadoes guarded stacks of fossils when they weren't getting drunk and fighting amongst themselves.

And the sensationalized headlines continued:

MARSH'S APATOSAURUS
LARGEST DINOSAUR EVER FOUND!

MASKED GUNMEN STEAL FOSSIL SHIPMENT!

EVEN BIGGER DINOSAUR DISCOVERED
COPE'S CAMARASAURUS!

MARSH CLAIMS TITANOSAURUS LARGEST DINOSAUR YET!

COPE CLAIMS CAMARASAURUS BIGGER THAN TITANOSAURUS!

DINOSAUR GOLDRUSH!

BONE BONANZA!

THE FOSSIL FEUD!

"The Fossil Feud? I like that!"

P. T. Barnum was puffing on a cigar in a cramped office teeming with circus memorabilia. He was holding a copy of the *New York Times* and grinning at the headline.

"Tom!" he shouted.

The office door opened and Tom Thumb entered. Barnum's diminutive friend and star attraction wore his signature costume, a miniature general's uniform.

"Yes, P. T.?"

"Do we have any newspaper friends in Wyoming?"

"We have newspaper friends everywhere," Tom replied. "The *Daily Sentinel* in Laramie has been kind to us in the past."

"Then we shall send a telegraph to the *Daily Sentinel* in Laramie!"

Rae Callahan sat alone at a table in the Como Bluff Saloon, sipping from a glass of whiskey. Dark rings beneath her eyes betrayed her exhaustion.

"Miss Callahan?"

She looked up with tired eyes. It was Marsh. "I thought that was you. Are you all right, my dear?"

"I didn't think you people ever stopped digging."

"I had some business with the local marshal. And quite honestly, I needed a break from the company of those outlaws we hired. I've never seen men spit so much."

She smiled at this.

"May I?" he asked, motioning to the empty chair beside her.

She nodded, and Marsh took a seat.

"You seem upset. Romantic troubles, I'll wager."

"Is there another kind?"

Marsh smiled kindly. "My dear. Much as I envy that beau of yours, he's a good man. Cope doesn't appreciate him."

"Sure and that's the truth. He's paying those outlaws twice what he's paying James."

"I'd be happy to give Mr. Garvey a job at twice his salary."

"James would never agree. He'd never betray Cope."

"Aren't you getting tired of the whole affair?"

She didn't answer.

"My offer still stands," he added.

She smiled and shook her head, but before she could speak, Marsh leaned over and kissed her gently. She didn't pull away. After a moment, he leaned back. Catching sight of something behind Rae, his eyes widened in surprise.

Rae spun around. Garvey stood in the doorway, watching them.

"James . . ." she began.

He turned and stormed off without saying a word. Rae stood to go after him, but Marsh grabbed her arm.

"You deserve better, Rae."

She looked at him for a moment, then pulled away and ran outside.

———

Rae caught Garvey before he could mount his horse.

"James, wait!"

"I don't want to hear it! None of it! I'm sick of your lies, Rae."

"There's nothing between us, James—"

Garvey scowled. "And why should I believe a lying whore like you?"

Rae slapped him across the face.

"You go to straight to hell."

She turned and saw Marsh standing by his carriage, watching.

"Does your offer still stand, Mr. Marsh?"

"Of course it does, my dear."

"Let's go, then."

As Marsh helped her into his carriage, Garvey shouted defiantly. "That's right. You go! And don't come back, neither!"

She couldn't even look at him. Marsh tugged on the reins and the carriage pulled away.

———

"I just can't believe it."

Garvey walked alongside Cope, telling him what

happened.

"She was manipulating you, Mr. Garvey," said Cope.

"Guess I didn't know her as well as I thought," Garvey replied.

"I guess none of us did."

Now Sternberg ran up to them, out of breath.

"Edward, you won't believe it!"

Cope, Garvey, and Sternberg approached the edge of the excavation pit as Carlin and his men stood around, grinning like fools.

"Look at them grinnin'," said Garvey. "You'd think they just discovered teeth."

Carlin's grin widened. "We discovered something better'n teeth, I reckon."

"This is it, Charles," said Cope. "This is the big one."

In the center of the pit lay the partially excavated skeleton of a long-necked, long-tailed dinosaur. It was gargantuan. Easily the largest skeleton found, to date.

"I've never seen anything this large!" said Sternberg.

Cope's eyes were bright with excitement. "No one has. Until now." He looked up at the grinning workers. "I'd say this calls for a celebration, wouldn't you, gentlemen?"

The entire group erupted in a cheer.

Chapter Twenty-Five

COMO BLUFF, WYOMING TERRITORY

Music from a four-man jug band wafted across the camp, which was now illuminated by a ring of torches set around the perimeter. The area around the rim of the excavation pit had been roped off to prevent any drunken diggers from stumbling into it. Cope had laid out a buffet and brought in a number of saloon girls to join the celebration.

In the center of the camp, in a place of honor atop a large wooden crate, sat the enormous skull from the most recent find.

Carlin and his men were already drunk and having a great time dancing, shouting, and intermittently firing their guns into the air. Cope and Sternberg were sitting near the skull, enjoying the festivities. Garvey sat with them, but didn't seem to be enjoying himself.

Cope noticed his frown. "Miss Callahan showed

you her true colors, Mr. Garvey. Be glad it happened sooner, and not later."

But Garvey was distracted by something behind Cope.

"Well, well. Look what's comin'."

Cope and Sternberg turned. Carlin, who had been dancing, reached over and picked up his rifle, which was never far out of his reach. He cocked it with a loud *clack-clack*. The band fell silent.

A large party approached on horseback: Marsh and the local marshal were in the lead, followed by Mudge, Lakes, and Rae Callahan. Reed and his desperadoes brought up the rear.

Carlin's men stepped forward, drawing and cocking their own weapons.

"Easy boys," said Reed, grinning. "Don't shoot the marshal. It's frowned upon."

Marsh nodded to Cope. "Edward."

Cope stood, defiantly. "This is a private party, O. C."

The marshal dismounted. "Are you Professor Edward Drinker Cope?"

"You know I am."

Garvey glared at Rae. She looked back at him, defiantly.

The marshal reached into his vest pocket, produced a folded document, and handed it to Cope.

Cope quickly glanced at it, nonplussed. "What's the meaning of this?"

"The meaning, my dear Edward, is that under the provisions of the Desert Land Act, I have purchased this entire area for twenty-five cents an acre. The purchase includes all natural resources, be they vegetable, mineral, or animal, living or dead."

The marshal continued. "You are hereby ordered to vacate the area immediately. Any animal skeletons still in the area are now the sole property of Professor O. C. Marsh."

Cope was shocked beyond belief.

"Now," said Marsh, "if you'd be so kind as to get off my land?"

Carlin raised his rifle. "You can't do this!"

The marshal cocked his own rifle. "We can. And we are."

Reed chuckled. "Looks like you backed the wrong horse, Carlin."

Carlin's face was flushed with anger, but he lowered his gun. Marsh smiled and climbed off his horse. He walked over to the huge skull, examining it.

"Astonishing. This could be the find of my career."

"This is despicable, Othniel!" shouted Cope.

Marsh shook his head in mock contrition. "It happens to be the law, Edward." Marsh looked to Garvey. "I'd like you to stay on with me, Mr. Garvey. I'll double your salary."

Garvey looked at Rae with a scowl.

"James, please . . ." said Rae.

Garvey spit in the dirt, and then looked up at her. "I already got a job."

"Suit yourself," said Marsh. "The offer stands, if you change your mind."

————

By noon the following morning, Cope and Garvey were already drunk.

They were sitting at a table in the Como Bluff Saloon. Carlin and his men were also there. They stood gathered in the center of the room where two of the desperadoes were playing a game with knives — circling with a piece of rawhide stretched between them, clenched in their teeth, they swung the blades at each other viciously. Carlin and others were drinking, placing bets, and cheering them on.

One of the men was nicked with his opponent's knife. He screamed in pain, released the rawhide, and jumped back. Money changed hands as the next two men prepared to play.

Cope watched the scene blearily. "I wonder if I could persuade Marsh to have a go at that."

"I know it stings," said Garvey, "but Marsh did follow the letter of law."

"Then the law be damned!" Cope scoffed. "This isn't about real estate, it's about science!"

"Science, huh?" said Garvey, downing a shot. "Is that all?"

"Of course."

Garvey didn't look convinced. "Seems to me that dinosaur's still gonna make the science books, no matter whose name's on it."

"Well, obviously it's not just about science," Cope admitted. "It's also about justice and fair play. I found that skeleton!"

"All by yourself, did you?"

Cope shot him a look. "You know exactly what I mean."

"Let me ask you something," said Garvey, refilling

their glasses. "If Marsh found the skeleton, and you were the one found that real estate loophole, do you think we'd still be havin' this conversation?"

"Bah!" Cope dismissed the thought without consideration.

Sternberg entered the saloon with a newspaper under his arm. He gave the knife game a wide berth and hurried over to their table.

"Edward," he whispered urgently, "have you seen this?"

He opened the paper and held it up. It was the latest edition of the *Daily Sentinel.* The headline read:

GREAT SHOWMAN P. T. BARNUM OFFERS $10,000 FOR GENUINE DINOSAUR SKELETON!

Cope's eyes went wide. "Good Lord."

"Indeed," said Sternberg. He looked over towards Carlin and his men, then lowered his voice even more. "I bought up all the local copies. I shudder to think what would happen if those outlaws were to see this."

Cope looked thoughtful for a moment, and then a sinister smile crossed his face.

"Who knows what mischief they'd get into."

Garvey shook his head. "Professor, I'm not sure I like where you're going with this."

Sternberg shared his apprehension. "Edward? Surely, you wouldn't—"

But Cope was already standing and raising his voice in mock outrage.

"*Ten thousand dollars!* Why, it's criminal! Absolutely criminal!"

The knife game came to a lurching halt as the desperadoes turned their attention on Cope.

"Edward . . ." Sternberg warned.

But Carlin was already on his way over. "What about ten thousand dollars?"

Cope snatched the paper off the table and hugged it to his chest.

"Why, nothing! Nothing at all."

"Edward," Sternberg whispered. "Don't do this!"

Carlin licked his lips and looked around at his men.

"Nuthin', huh? Then you wouldn't mind showin' us that newspaper?"

Cope stood. "I'm sorry, Mr. Carlin. I really must be going."

Sternberg grabbed his hat. "Yes, at once!"

Sternberg and Garvey grabbed Cope by either arm and rushed him towards the door, but the seed was already planted. Carlin intercepted them and snatched the paper.

"Now, see here!" said Cope in mock outrage.

Carlin looked at the headline, and then held it up for his men to see.

"Look here, boys. This big circus man is offerin' ten thousand dollars for a dinosaur!"

"A complete dinosaur skeleton," Cope corrected. "All of mine have been shipped to Philadelphia."

"Except for that big one we found this afternoon," said Carlin.

"It's no longer mine, remember? Legally, it belongs to Professor Marsh."

"Well, that don't seem right," Carlin said with a grin. "He best keep a close eye on it. Some bunch of crazy thieves might just steal it from him. Ain't that right, boys?"

He pulled out his pistols and fired them into the ceiling.

"Who's riding with me?"

The drunken desperadoes whooped it up as they followed Carlin out of the saloon.

Garvey wheeled on Cope. "You're playin' with fire, Cope! Those men are killers!"

Cope looked unsure. "Marsh has it coming to him."

"And Rae, and Artie Lakes? They got it coming, too?"

Garvey shook his head, adjusted his gun belt, and left the saloon.

Cope turned to Sternberg, looking for reassurance. "You must understand, Charles."

Sternberg shook his head. "No, Edward. Not this."

Sternberg ran to catch up to Garvey, but before he could reach the door, gunfire erupted outside.

Garvey stood in the middle of the train tracks firing his gun as Carlin and the desperadoes raced off on horseback. Sternberg and Cope appeared from the saloon.

"We'll go after them!" said Sternberg.

"On what, Charlie?" said Garvey. "They took our horses!"

Chapter Twenty-Six

COMO BLUFF, WYOMING TERRITORY

Arthur Lakes sat before his artist's easel looking out over the field of partially excavated bones. The sun was beginning to set and he was taking advantage of the last rays of golden light to put the finishing touches on another watercolor painting of the dig. As he dabbed paint on the canvas he hummed quietly to himself.

Suddenly, a shot rang out and a bullet-sized hole pierced the canvas. Lakes froze for a moment, in shocked disbelief, and then fell to the dirt as more shots peppered the area around him. He looked up fearfully as Carlin and his men roared past him on horseback.

Reed rushed across the encampment, shouting orders to his men. They grabbed their rifles and began to return fire. One of Carlin's men took a bullet in the chest and fell from his saddle, screaming in pain.

Marsh and the town marshal stepped out of the

main tent.

"What's happening?" Marsh shouted.

The marshal saw one of the attackers riding towards them, raising his rifle. He reached for his own sidearm, but wasn't fast enough. The rider fired and the marshal went down, blood spiraling from his chest.

Marsh sidestepped, drew his own long-barreled pistol, and fired. The rider was knocked from his saddle and fell to the ground, motionless. Marsh spun to see Rae emerging from her tent.

"Miss Callahan!" he shouted. "Run for the bluff!"

She grabbed the hem of her skirt and began to run.

Another of the attackers, Noonan, an ugly pinched-faced man with a pockmarked face, spun his horse and galloped after her. He caught Rae in the crook of his arm and threw her, screaming, over his saddle.

Carlin waved his gun and shouted to two more of his men. "Get Marsh!"

The two riders galloped towards Marsh. Marsh fired, his shot going wide. The first man returned fire, catching Marsh in the shoulder, while the other swung a wide loop of rope, encircling Marsh and pulling him off his feet.

Reed fired in one direction, then the other, but there were too many riders and his men were falling all around him. He heard a familiar voice from behind him.

"I told you you'd get yours, you son of a bitch."

Reed turned. Carlin stood right behind him, rifle raised.

Reed dropped his pistol and raised his arms.

"Don't do it."

Carlin smiled and fired, point-blank. Reed caught the shot in the stomach, and dropped instantly.

Now the desperadoes galloped by the fire pit, igniting torches as they passed, and began setting fire to the tents. Within moments, the entire encampment was in flames.

"Get the bones!" Carlin shouted.

———

Hours later, Garvey, Sternberg, and Cope reached the smoldering remains of the camp riding three broken-down old mules they had rented from a local prospector. As they approached, Lakes peered fearfully from cover behind one of the smoldering tents. He saw them and lowered his rifle, relieved.

"Thank God."

"Are you okay, Mr. Lakes?" Garvey asked.

"I was lucky," he replied. "But they killed the marshal and all of the hired men."

Garvey jumped down from his horse and looked at Lakes, his face ashen. "What about Rae?"

"They took her. And the professor as well. They also took the skeleton."

"I'm so sorry," said Cope. "I didn't think—"

"No," said Garvey. "You didn't think. That's the point."

Now, the unmistakable sound of a muffled moan reached them. Garvey turned and approached another pile of rubble. He lifted several pieces of wood and threw them aside. Reed lay beneath, barely clinging to life.

Garvey took a knee beside him. "Reed," he said. "They got Marsh and Rae. Where would Carlin take them?"

Reed coughed painfully. "I . . . I don't know. There's an old farmhouse . . . near the North Platte River . . . just south of the crossing. We . . . used it as a hideout sometimes."

Garvey nodded. "We'll get you to a doctor."

"No," said Reed, weakly. "I'm gut shot. Can't even feel my legs." He coughed again, and blood tricked from the side of his mouth. "You got any whiskey?"

Lakes produced a flask. Garvey looked up at him, surprised. Lakes shrugged.

"I use it to thin the paint."

"I bet you do," said Garvey.

Garvey took the flask and bent to offer it to Reed, but Reed's eyes were already wide and lifeless. Garvey closed the dead man's eyes and then raised the flask in a toast.

"Here's to you, Reed."

He drank and handed the flask back to Lakes. He stood and looked around, examining the horse tracks in the mud.

"They'll be easy to track, but these mules ain't worth a damn. I need a horse."

"We'll need more than one," said Lakes, with a touch of anger and growing confidence.

"Yes," said Cope, in the same tone. "*We* will."

"Indeed," Sternberg added.

Garvey looked at this determined but unlikely posse.

"There's no law, now the marshal's dead. It's just us. And trust me, before it's over, it's gonna get bloody. You ride with me, you might not come back. Even if you do survive, you're gonna have to do some killin'.

Are you ready for that? Cause if you ain't, I don't want you along."

Cope's jaw was set. "I'm ready," he said.

"As am I," Lakes added.

Garvey turned to Sternberg. "How 'bout you, Charlie? Ready to shoot some bad guys?"

Sternberg spun his pistol expertly and holstered it. "Indeed."

"All right, then. Let's go find us some real horses."

They began to walk towards the mules.

Garvey grinned at Sternberg. "Indeed," he repeated. "That's about your favorite word isn't it?"

Before he could reply, Cope and Lakes answered for him, in unison.

"Indeed!"

Chapter Twenty-Seven

NORTH PLATTE RIVER, WYOMING TERRITORY

Zeke and Merle, two of Carlin's desperadoes, stood guard on the porch of a dilapidated two-story farmhouse, occasionally chugging from a large bottle of moonshine. The front door had fallen off its hinges and four more men were visible inside, playing cards at a table and getting drunk. A ramshackle barn stood a short distance from the house, lantern light flickering in its windows.

Inside the barn, Rae was assisting Marsh as he attempted to assemble the enormous skeleton. Marsh raised a piece of bone to wire it into place and winced at the effort. His shoulder wound was bandaged and leaking fresh blood.

"Hurry it up, old man," said Carlin. He and Noonan stood watching, and covering them with loaded rifles. An old-style photographic plate camera sat on a tripod nearby.

Marsh shook his head. "This is impossible. Why assemble it here?"

"I need a photographic picture to send to Barnum. We'll be ten thousand dollars richer soon enough, ain't that right, Noonan?"

Noonan chugged from a whiskey bottle and grinned, exposing yellow, tobacco-stained teeth.

"I'm countin' on it."

"Let's just do as they say, O. C.," said Rae, helping him hold the bone in position while he twisted wire around it.

Noonan leaned in and spoke to Carlin in a low tone.

"They seen our faces. They know we killed that marshal."

Carlin looked back at Marsh and Rae. They were preoccupied and didn't hear him. "Ssssh. Don't worry. Once the picture's taken, we'll get rid of them. We've taken enough bones out of the ground. I reckon it's time we put a few back."

Noonan chuckled menacingly.

Cope and his makeshift posse were making their way across the plains on four fresh horses, hoping to locate the hideout that Reed had mentioned.

"These are fine horses," Sternberg remarked. "Wouldn't it be ironic if we rescued them only to be hung as horse thieves?"

"I left a note with a reasonably sensible explanation," said Lakes.

Garvey shook his head. "I doubt if that old livery

man's an accomplished reader. But I wouldn't worry none. We'll probably all get shot, anyhow."

Lakes swallowed nervously. "You're not a very optimistic chap, are you?"

Cope's horse was bringing up the rear. He was still wracked with guilt and growing impatient.

"Can't we move any faster?" he said.

"We're moving too fast as it is," said Garvey. "I already lost the track twice. We can't afford no more doubling back."

Cope's face was ashen. "You were right, Mr. Garvey," he said. "I've done a terrible thing."

"You won't get no argument from me on that."

"I couldn't help myself. My damnable pride got the better of me."

Garvey smiled grimly. "Well, finally!"

"What?"

"Professor, you made a mistake. A big mistake. And that mistake weren't about science, or justice, or none of that claptrap. It was about pride. Foolish pride. And that's the first time I've heard you say it."

"I'd give anything to change what happened."

"Well, lettin' the cat out of the bag's a whole lot easier than puttin' her back in." Garvey fell silent for a moment, and then added, "You once told me that good judgment comes from experience, and experience mostly comes from bad judgment. The important thing is, now you're doing right. Whatever the outcome, you're learning from your missteps. That's somethin', at least."

"It doesn't make it any easier."

"No, I expect it don't. Life ain't fair, but it ain't fair

for everybody. I reckon that makes life fair, in the long drive."

———————

Merle was leaning back in a porch rocking chair, snoring loudly. Zeke was sitting on the front steps with his back to Merle, picking his nose industriously. Inside, the card game continued.

Suddenly, a hand slipped over Merle's mouth and the moonlight flashed on a metal blade at his throat.

Zeke spoke without turning.

"I never thought you'd stop that snorin', Merle."

When there was no response, Zeke turned to look at his partner. Merle's chair was empty, but still rocking slightly.

"Merle?"

Zeke stood and drew his pistol. Slowly, he crept towards the side of the house, gun raised. "Dammit Merle, are you pissin' or what?"

Zeke rounded the corner of the house and stopped in his tracks. Merle was lying against the side of the house, eyes wide, blood pulsing from the slash across his throat.

"Merle!"

Now a figure leapt from the roof of the porch on to Zeke's back, flattening him. It was Garvey. Zeke spun wildly, firing his pistol into the air before falling dead with Garvey's knife buried in his throat.

At the sound of the shot, the men inside the house looked up from their cards.

Instantly, Sternberg kicked the back door open and

stepped through with a pistol in each hand. Cope and Lakes were right behind him. The cardplayers leapt to their feet, hands reaching for their pistols, but they froze when they saw that Sternberg had the advantage.

"As you were, gentlemen."

––––––––

Inside the barn, Carlin looked up at the sound of Zeke's shot.

"What in hell was that?" He turned to Noonan. "Watch them!" He grabbed his rifle and headed out of the barn.

As soon as he was out of sight, Noonan turned and eyed Rae with undisguised lust.

"I'll do more than watch," the outlaw muttered. "You're pretty as a red heifer in a flower bed, missy. C'mere and give me a kiss."

She held up one of the fossil bones, defensively. "Go straight to hell."

"Woo-hoo! You got a mouth on you, don't you?" Noonan approached menacingly. "It's gettin' me all excited, you want the truth."

Marsh stepped between them.

"Stay away from her."

Noonan punched Marsh in the stomach, then backhanded him across the face, sending him sprawling.

Rae swung the bone and smashed the outlaw across the temple. He stumbled backwards.

––––––––

"One at a time," said Sternberg, waving his pistol

at the stunned cardplayers. "Take your guns from their holsters and drop them on the table." He motioned to the largest man. "You first."

The big man looked to the man across from him, who nodded slightly, then winked. Now all four cardplayers went for their guns simultaneously.

Sternberg opened fire, killing the big man instantly. Lakes killed another, but Cope's shot went wild, as usual. The fourth man spun and fired his own pistol, catching Lakes in the arm.

Carlin was halfway to the house when the gunfire erupted. He cocked his rifle and slipped into the shadows at the side of the house, then peered out.

Garvey was running past him to the front door, rifle raised.

Garvey leapt through the front door, firing his rifle. Another of the two remaining cardplayers took it in the chest. The last man upended the card table and dropped behind it. Garvey fired three more times, peppering the tabletop.

"Where are they?" he shouted.

The frightened voice of the cardplayer came from behind the table.

"In the barn!"

Hearing this, Cope slipped out the back door, unnoticed.

Now, two more men came rushing down the stairs from the second floor.

Garvey spun and fired, killing the first. The second backed into the shadows for cover, then fired at Garvey, pinning him against a wall. Garvey shouted to Sternberg and Lakes.

"Where's Cope?"

Sternberg and Lakes turned. Cope was gone.

"Professor?" shouted Sternberg.

Garvey was pressed flat against the wall as bullets peppered the plaster around him. "Cope can't shoot for shit!" Garvey shouted. "Go after him!"

Sternberg and Lakes nodded and rushed out the back door.

Garvey took a deep breath, and then leapt out, firing up the stairs. His rounds caught the second man in the chest and he tumbled down the stairs, landing with his limbs twisted at impossible angles.

The remaining cardplayer was still hiding behind the table, trying to work up the nerve to attack. Garvey approached slowly with his gun raised.

There was a deafening crash as Carlin came through a side window, shattering it. He fired his rifle at Garvey, repeatedly. Garvey leapt and rolled, narrowly escaping the rounds.

The cardplayer stood up, turning his gun on Garvey. Carlin caught sight of his shadow, pivoted around and fired, killing his own man.

"Shit!" shouted Carlin.

Now Garvey stood up. "You're empty, Carlin."

Carlin spun his rifle back and pulled the trigger, but the hammer fell on an empty chamber. He tossed the rifle aside and raised his arms.

Garvey had one round left in his own rifle, and the barrel was pointed at Carlin's chest.

———————

Inside the barn, Marsh lay on the floor, bleeding. Rae dropped the bone she'd used to club Noonan and rushed over to help Marsh.

Noonan struggled to his feet, dazed from the blow to the head, but not down for the count. He looked around wildly and spotted an axe hanging on the wall of the barn. He snatched it and approached Rae and Marsh, his eyes blazing with rage. He raised the axe above his head with both arms, ready to strike down at them. Marsh looked up at him, defiantly. Rae closed her eyes, bracing for the blow.

A shot rang out and a bullet splintered a wooden post inches from Noonan's head. Professor Cope was standing a few feet away, holding his trembling pistol with both hands.

"Put it down," said Cope.

The outlaw grinned. "I don't think so."

Cope fired again, the shot going wide. Noonan rushed at him, swinging the axe, but Cope sidestepped, avoiding the blow but taking the larger man's shoulder in the chest. Cope was slammed backwards into the wall, the pistol knocked from his grasp.

Now the two men wrestled with the axe. Noonan caught Cope's chin with his elbow, and Cope fell to the floor. The outlaw raised the axe, preparing to bring it down on Cope's skull. Cope's eyes grew wide.

Another shot rang out. Noonan teetered for a moment with a surprised look on his face. A thin trickle of blood traveled down the side of his nose from a hole in the center of his forehead. After a long moment, he collapsed to the barn floor and lay dead.

Cope turned. Marsh stood a few feet away, holding Cope's smoking pistol. Cope gulped with relief, and then nodded.

"Othniel."

"Edward."

Sternberg and Lakes rushed in behind Cope, guns at the ready, then held up, surprised to see that the job had already been done.

———

Carlin stood in the living room of the farmhouse, grinning, with his hands held high.

"You gonna shoot me in cold blood?'

"No," said Garvey, lowering his rifle and leaning it against an overturned chair. He took a step forward, facing Carlin, and stood with his hand poised above his pistol.

Carlin's eyes narrowed. His fingers twitched over his own pistols. The two stood, eyes locked on each other, for an endless moment.

Carlin went for his guns.

Garvey's draw was faster. Before Carlin could get off a shot, a hole appeared in his chest. He dropped to his knees and teetered, a surprised look on his face. Then his eyes rolled back, and he fell forward, dead.

———

By the time Garvey got to the barn, Rae and Sternberg

were binding Lakes's wound.

"Mr. Garvey!" said Lakes. "Did any of them get away?"

Garvey shook his head. "I reckon they've gone extinct."

Rae threw her arms around Garvey and he returned her embrace, enthusiastically.

Cope turned and looked up at the nearly assembled dinosaur skeleton.

"Have you named her yet, O. C.?" he asked.

"She's rightfully yours, Edward."

"You're damned right she is."

Garvey shot Cope a warning look.

"But," Cope continued, "there will be others. And bigger than this. You'll see." He put his hand on Marsh's shoulder. "I'd like you to keep her."

Marsh was stunned. "Are you sure?"

"Quite sure."

Garvey grinned broadly.

"I don't know what to say!" said Marsh. "Thank you, Edward. I'll give her a place of honor at the museum."

"So," Cope repeated, "what about a name?"

"I thought *Brontosaurus excelsus*." Cope nodded in approval. "Thunder lizard. Excellent."

"Indeed," Sternberg added.

⁂

The entire saloon sat silently enraptured as Garvey finished his tale.

"So, in the end, Cope let Marsh have the Brontosaurus

skeleton. Marsh set it up at Yale, right in the main hall of the Peabody Museum."

I couldn't help but ask, "What happened to the woman? Rae Callahan?"

A female voice with an unmistakably Irish accent answered from across the room.

"Why, she married him, of course!"

We all turned to see a figure standing in the doorway. Her red hair was streaked with gray, but she was still as lovely and as full of life as I'd imagined. This had to be Rae.

"Twice," Garvey added. "First time didn't take. She ran off with a riverboat captain and moved to Louisiana, of all places. Couldn't stay away long, though."

Rae walked over and kissed him.

"He has a short rope," she said with a wink, "but he throws a wide loop."

I stood, offering my seat, which she accepted with a curtsy. She treated herself to the whiskey in my glass, downing it in one shot. I liked her immediately.

"So, that was the end of the feud?" I asked.

"Oh, no," said Garvey. "It goes on, even today. But it ain't bein' fought in the field no more. It's in the scientific journals, the museums, and the classrooms."

"There's something I don't get, Garv," said one of the cardplayers. "Why did Cope let Marsh have the dinosaur skeleton? He found it. Seems like it was his by rights."

"Well now, I've often puzzled over that myself," said Garvey. "I suppose because he felt guilty about the attack on the camp."

The cardplayer shrugged. "Sounds plausible, I guess."

"Well, there's another theory I got, but I'm no expert, so I can't confirm it." Garvey turned to me, his voice growing serious. "And this ain't for printing, neither. I'll deny it up and down."

I nodded and closed my notebook. "Off the record, then."

"Off the record?" Garvey leaned back in his chair and was silent for a long moment, letting our anticipation build. "I was there the day we found them bones," he said, finally. "We found a complete skeleton, all right. It was perfect, in all ways but one."

"What was wrong with it?" I asked.

❦

It was the day of the initial discovery. Cope was walking down the earthen ramp into the excavation pit carrying something large, wrapped in burlap. He approached Sternberg and Garvey and all three looked down at the enormous, unearthed skeleton. It was headless.

"There's no skull here, Professor," said Sternberg. "It's perfect in all respects, but there's no skull."

"Yes, I know," said Cope.

He set the wrapped bundle on the ground beside the skeleton and carefully unwrapped it. It was a large dinosaur skull.

"This should do nicely. It was found in quarry three," he said. "It looks to be the same species."

Garvey shrugged. "Works for me."

"That skull was from another quarry, a mile away," Garvey explained. "It couldn't have been the same animal. Cope thought it might be the same species, but he never had time to check. To know for sure."

Slowly, I began to understand.

Epilogue

Months after the events came to a head at Como Bluff, Cope, Marsh, and Joseph Leidy, the paleontologist who was present at the unveiling of Cope's "wrong-headed dinosaur" all those years ago, stood before the polished, reconstructed skeleton. It sat in a place of honor in the center of the great hall at the Peabody Museum at Yale University. Marsh was beaming proudly. Leidy looked suitably impressed.

Cope was also smiling, but there was a knowing twinkle in his eye.

The inscription on a brass plate beneath the skeleton read:

BRONTOSAURUS EXCELSUS

⚜

"It's my belief," Garvey explained, "that Cope knew it wasn't right. And, since Marsh assumed the skull was found with the rest, I don't think he gave it a second thought."

Garvey cracked his knuckles.

"Wouldn't it be something," he continued, "if Cope had one last joke on old Marsh? If that Brontosaurus skeleton, the pride of Yale University, was a bigger humbug than anything in P. T. Barnum's sideshow? Wouldn't that just beat all?"

⚜

Nearly one hundred years after its discovery, evidence proved that the fossil remains of Marsh's *Brontosaurus excelsus* were actually those of *Apatosaurus ajax*, a dinosaur Marsh had previously discovered and named. Cope had placed the head of a *Camarasaurus* on an *Apatosaurus* skeleton and Marsh wrongly assumed them to be a new species.

The error was discovered in 1970 by two scientists, John McIntosh from Wesleyan University and David Berman of the Carnegie Museum of Natural History. In 1974 the name *Brontosaurus* was formally discarded by paleontologists worldwide.

To this day, the skeleton bears a nameplate that reads *Brontosaurus excelsus*.

The End

RESTORATION OF
BRONTOSAURUS EXCELSUS

American Journal of Science, 1883

BY O.C. MARSH

About the Author

Wynne McLaughlin was born in Salem, Massachusetts and currently resides in New Freedom, Pennsylvania with his wife, Cathy, and their three crazy dogs. Wynne is a video game designer, screenwriter, and television writer. He is a member of the Writer's Guild of America, west and the International Game Developers Association. This is his first novel.

You can contact the author on:

FACEBOOK
facebook.com/wynnemclaughlin.author

TWITTER
twitter.com/SpacemanQuisp/

GOODREADS
goodreads.com/author/show/9760829.Wynne_McLaughlin

Made in the USA
San Bernardino, CA
27 June 2017